THE WANDERPEOPLE

by

JP Wagner

THE WANDERPEOPLE

First edition. March 1, 2023.

ISBN: 978-1-990862-10-6

Written by J P Wagner.
Edited by Beth Wagner

Dedication

I'd like to thank Sarah and Lila, your support has meant the world to me.

Introduction

Thank you for purchasing this book. I was not as familiar with this book as I had been with the others that I worked on so far. But I found the concept intriguing, a group of nomadic Barbarians and their struggle to survive.

CONTENT WARNING: This book contains adult themes of an upsetting nature and may not be for everyone. Not recommended for people under the age of 18.

1. The City

The wagons rolled up toward the place where the city of Dannon-ska stood tall and stark out of the Plains. It was a large city, with high walls mostly of baked mud-brick, though some of it was built of blue-white stone brought at great expense from the far-off mountains.

The wagons rolled on, great heavy things on spoked wheels tall as a man, with their attendant cloud of dust both displaying their presence from afar and masking their numbers as they drew close.

Around the wagons were the hordes of cattle, the horses and dogs and even the laughing children of the Wanderpeople, the people who lived on the Great Mother Plain.

"Pah! There he stands again!" Grannon poked his chin off towards the small rise of ground before the city where the King of the City sat on his horse. Grannon looked down at his son, Fatha. "We shall have to deal with him, as we have always dealt with him. And in the days when I am gone, Fatha, it will be for you to deal with him. Come."

The two directed their horses toward the hillock where the King sat. There were great similarities and differences between the two Wanderpeople and the King of Dannon-ska. All of them had jet-black hair and dark brown eyes, all of them had naturally light-brown skin, all of them had powerful physiques.

But the King was more slender in build than Grannon or Fatha, and his skin was not further browned by the sun of the Plains. His hair and beard were oiled and elaborately curled, and his eyelashes carefully painted darker than their natural black.

As for Grannon and Fatha, their hair and beards were straight, the hair pulled back and bound behind the head with a plain thong of leather. Their clothing consisted of well-worn and serviceable leather jackets and trousers, whereas the King wore robes of coloured silk over a breastplate of gold. The King's sword was so heavily decorated with gems and gold that it was no longer useable as a weapon. Grannon and Fatha carried plain swords in leather sheaths, as well as a cased bow and arrows slung from each saddle, under the rider's right leg.

The two Wanderpeople were also marked on the right cheek, as was common with every adult of their band, with a small brand in the shape of a flower with triangular petals. The face of the King of Dannon-ska was smooth and unmarked. As they neared the King, another horseman appeared behind him. The horseman dressed in much the same fashion, but with a trifle less magnificence. Behind him were two ranks of foot soldiers, men wearing leather breastplates and carrying large round shields, with swords belted at their waists. These soldiers arrayed themselves in the path of the two men and waited.

The well-dressed noble waited until they were close enough that he need not raise his voice unduly to be heard. "Halt! Who approaches?"

Grannon answered. "I am Grannon, Chief of the Wanderpeople, and this is my son, Fatha." Under his breath, he muttered to Fatha, "As if we have not been making this same journey every year of the twenty years since my father died."

"No one approaches the King of Dannon-ska save afoot."

Without a word, Grannon dismounted, and Fatha followed suit. With practised ease, the soldiers of the city changed their formation so that they formed a lane of two ranks of men leading up to where the King sat. The two Wanderpeople walked forward to approach the King. The noble rode up to the King and whispered to him.

There was now a person standing beside the King's horse, a little man with greying hair, wearing an ordinary linen robe. The King spoke, and this man then put his words into the language of the Wanderpeople. There was little need for this, for the two languages were very nearly one and the same, but it was a conceit of the City People that the Plainsfolk were rude, crude, barbarous, and spoke an incomprehensible dialect.

"What do you do in our territory, Wanderpeople?"

"We only pass through, O King, may you live forever." Grannon said all of this, giving no sign that he resented having to humble himself. Fatha, however, knew what it cost his father.

"What will you offer us that we should allow you to pass through our territory?"

"O King, whose splendour is as the sun, we offer thirty of our best cattle, along with a hundred cured hides, and one pound of gold."

The King appeared to consider this, though they had fixed it by treaty long ago. Finally he said, "It is enough. Have the goods delivered to my servants. Camp no more than two nights in one place, and see that your people steal nothing from my people. You are dismissed."

Without waiting for anything the two might say in reply, he swung his horse around and rode away. The lord spoke a few sharp words of command and rode away himself, followed shortly by the soldiers. Grannon and Fatha returned to their horses and mounted.

"By the toes of the Clan-spirit!" Grannon burst out. "Each year, they become more presumptuous! It would be good sometime to tear down their walls and show them what their city is worth!"

Fatha nodded. "We have the numbers to do so."

Quickly, as his rage had mounted, Grannon mastered it. "We have the numbers to do so, but the cost of tearing down those walls would be the weakening of our Clan. And once our Clan was weakened, there are too many others on the Plain who would take advantage of our weakness."

Fatha nodded again. "What that means is that we ought to make an alliance with one or two of the other Wanderpeople Clans to attack the city."

Grannon smiled. "Alliances there have been, alliances there will be, but I do not yet think that our injured pride will be sufficient cause to make such an alliance; a war such as that is not lightly waged, Fatha."

They rode back to the wagons, where already men were sending out the long-prepared tribute.

2. The Wagons

Fatha made his way to a particular wagon which bore on the sides of the hide cover a painting of a red rose superimposed on a sunburst. As he rode, he waved and called a word here and there to young people on his path; only a few noticed that most of these people were young women.

Seeing him approach, a young woman dropped lightly from the tail of the wagon and came running up. Her long hair was black, her complexion was brown as any of the Plainsfolk, but her face was a little more slender, her features a little more fine. She wore a long leather skirt with a blouse of black cloth. Woven clothing had become more common among the Wanderpeople in recent years, though most still held by leather.

"Ah, Naro!" He called. "How goes it this morning?"

Narolen laughed. "Ah, Fiyo! Best be careful about using pet-names so close to the wagon! My father will have us sworn and married before you can blink!"

He chuckled in return, extending an arm which she grasped, and swung her up onto the horse behind him. Then he looked back at her.

"And if he sees you riding behind me all the time, what then, Naro?"

Her eyes danced. "It is you, not I, who wants to avoid marriage, Fiyo!"

Suddenly, her face went serious. Fatha followed her glance and saw his stepmother looking out over the tail of their own wagon. She was ten years older than Fatha, old enough for an older sister, hardly old enough for a mother, and Fatha had never felt easy around her. It was partly due to this that he had finally badgered his father into helping him make his own wagon.

"She still worries you, Naro? Listen, she married my father because she felt it would give her a position of power and influence among the people. Now that she has discovered that my father is influenced only when he lets himself be influenced, she has begun to feel frustrated, and her temper suffers. But Bougil is harmless."

Naro shook her head. "Fiyo, you are too trusting, too easygoing. She hates you!"

Fatha laughed. "Hate? I think not. I think rather she wishes she had married me, since she feels that I, being younger, could more easily be bent to her will when my father dies and I succeed him as chief." He laughed again at the thought of marrying her.

Narolen looked doubtful. "She visits with Yopan, the shaman, very often."

"And Yopan is not one of my father's greatest supporters, since he also wishes for more power and influence among the people. But in fact, she has come to feel that she would have more influence if she could bear a son for my father, which she has so far been unable to do. So, of course, she has been visiting the shaman.

"Now let us talk about other more important things, such as whether your eyes are more beautiful when they are green, as now, or when they are brown, as they become when the light is different."

She laughed. "And to how many other girls have you told that?"

"None at all!" he protested.

"Ah, then you have just thought it up?"

"Naro, can you not believe that my love is for you alone?"

"For me, and for any other girl who will return your smile." But she herself was smiling as she said it.

"Let us ride a little out to the outskirts, where the dust is not so bad."

"But not for too long, Fiyo. My father will be concerned."

"Not for long."

They rode out a little from the wagons. It would have required a long distance to get beyond the sound of the squeaking wagons, the bawling cattle, the shouts of the children, but at least they were out of the worst of the dust.

There was a wagon rolling along on a parallel course to theirs, far off on the plain. Fatha frowned. "Outcast!" he muttered.

He felt Narolen shudder. "There is nothing to fear, Naro. They will not approach our wagons, not during the day. But I shall have to warn the herdsmen to be careful tonight."

"No, no, it was not that. I was only imagining how it must be to be an outcast, to have your Clan-mark slashed through and through, to have no more family, no more friends, to have every person in the world against you. Better to be dead instead!"

Fatha shrugged. "What else could we do with those who seriously disturb the peace of the Clan? To slay a fellow-clansman is a great horror, and yet for some crimes no lesser punishment will do. So the criminal is no longer a part of the Clan, with three days to go beyond the territory of the Clan. After that, he is slain if he is found; they say few survive long, even if no one goes hunting them."

Narolen shuddered again. "It is still a terrible thought."

They rode along in silence for a little, then Narolen said,

"Perhaps we had better be going back to the wagons. My father trusts you, Fiyo, but not all that much."

They rode back into the mass of wagons, finally finding the wagon of Narolen's father. As Fatha swung his horse in behind the wagon, Narolen jumped down lightly from the horse, ran up behind the wagon, caught the backboard, and vaulted in. Once inside, she turned and gave Fatha a wave and a smile. Answering her with a wave and a smile of his own, he turned his horse and rode to his own wagon.

Because of his youth, he was not yet permitted to decorate his wagon-cover, but even so, he could find his wagon quickly. Also, due to his youth, he was required to keep his wagon to the rear, in the dust of the elders.

As many people did from time to time, he had arranged for a young boy to drive his wagon for the morning while he was with his father and doing other business. Scarcely more than a child, the boy was carefully watching the oxen in their yokes. He was very conscious of the responsibility placed on him, and somewhat fearful lest one of the beasts break his leg in a hole, or lest the wagon roll over too great a hump or stone and break a wheel.

"Ah, Gily! All goes well?"

"All goes well, Fatha. Will you be driving now?"

"Yes, I'll drive for a little now, and you can rest. You have done well."

The boy beamed with pride at the compliment. He looked around. "Is it all right if I ride here for a while? My father's wagon will be way up ahead."

"Certainly. I'll just tie my horse to the tail of the wagon, then I'll take the reins."

Shortly after that, Fatha was seated at the front of the wagon beside Gily. They had been riding thus only a little while when Grannon came riding up out of the dust.

"Ah, Fiyo! I must talk to you."

"Ah, Father! Will you ride in my wagon for a bit, then?"

Grannon swung himself easily from the back of his horse to the seat of the wagon, then tied his horse's reins to one of the wagon-posts. He looked at Gily. "Gily, I must talk to Fatha alone."

Fatha glanced at Gily. "Gily, go back and ride my horse while father and I talk."

The boy's face lit up. "You mean it, Fatha?"

"If I didn't mean it, I would not have said it. Go on and be careful with him."

When Gily had gone, father and son rode in silence for a time until finally Grannon spoke. "The best way to say it, I suppose, is to come out and say it. Be careful how you deal with the girls, Fatha."

"Oh, they all know I mean no harm, father. And I am careful to do nothing improper."

Grannon nodded. "And for most young men of your age that would be sufficient, and there would be no need to worry. But you are my son, and should be heir to the leadership when I die. And that means that propriety and impropriety for you may be measured a little more strictly.

"You have five uncles, you know, all married to my sisters, all men who see themselves as possible Clan-chieftains. None of them has sufficient support to challenge you for the leadership, but one or two dissatisfied fathers might just tip the balance, for they would carry with them the support of several brothers, uncles, and cousins."

"I hear, father."

"It might be best if you were married, but that would be thrusting you too soon into the state, which would not make for a good marriage. Not to mention that it would be a complicated political choice to get you the right bride whose family would do you the most good, or at worst, do you the least harm."

"And I am not yet ready to settle down with one woman."

Grannon shot him a look. "The time may come when you may have to do things, whether you are ready for them or not."

"Yes, father. But I promise you I will be more careful in my dealings with the young women. If only to spare you the trouble of deciding who it is most convenient for me to marry."

"Good." Grannon ignored the gentle sarcasm. "And while we are talking, be very careful of old Naucles' younger daughter. I know you have already promised me you will be careful, but you have been showing a little extra attention in that direction, and all it would need would be the wrong word at the wrong time and you would be betrothed in his eyes. And there is little to be gained from a marriage there, my son."

Fatha looked up at his father. "You know, Naro was saying something the same to me this morning."

Grannon looked a little surprised. "She was? Well, she has more of a head on her shoulders than I would have thought."

They rode on in silence as Fatha thought to himself how times had changed. Once his father had told him tales of the cities of the Plain, of the cattle-raids between the people, of the wars between the cities. He had also told of the Goodly Ones and the strange lands in which they lived. Now, instead of warning Fatha against offending the Goodly Ones of the

Water, he warns him against offending his own clan.

And just as the most ordinary thing might be taken badly by the Goodly Ones of the Water, so apparently might the most ordinary action cause dissension among the people of the clan.

For an instant he felt a dreadful loneliness, a longing for his father to tell him once again of Glatha who had gone to the land of the Goodly Ones to aid in their wars and had returned with weapons of great magic. He shook himself; he was too old for such things now; as a man, he must deal with the problems of a man and not a child.

3. Raid!

Fatha rode quietly around the edge of the herd, the alarm-horn bumping lightly against his hip. Nine times out of ten there was no trouble with the herds, but on that tenth time, beware! Cattle-raiders might come, or wolves or some other beast of the Plains frighten the cattle into running.

If the cattle ran for whatever cause, the main thing to be done was to stay in front and turn the ones in the lead; the others would follow them, eventually settling down into a heaving mass of animals who, though still afraid, were no longer running.

If it were raiders, then those who bore the alarm-horns would sound them, again and again, to bring every able-bodied man from the wagons to help beat off the attack.

In the five years since he had first been sent out to watch the night herd, Fatha had only once had to deal with a raid, but numerous times had had to handle stampedes. Three years ago they had felt him old enough to carry an alarm-horn, and at first he had felt the weight of the responsibility heavily. Now, however, it was merely one more thing to remember.

His bow was strung in the bow-case; ordinarily, one would not leave a bow strung for long periods of time lest the bow be damaged, but on the night-herd there might not be time to string the bow when something happened. Of course, the bow was of limited use at night. When raiders came, the guards were more likely to use swords against them.

On this night, the moon was shining brightly, and a bow might be useful.

He rode over to where Grifa sat on his horse. Grifa was shorter and stockier than the general run of the Wanderpeople, and he also liked his food a little more, so he was a little husky, which on his heavy frame made him look very overweight. He was very good-natured, though, and something of a flashy dresser, occasionally starting fads of dress that spread gradually throughout the Clan. At present, for instance, he had taken to wearing a dyed feather knotted into a small braid of hair beside his right ear.

"Ah, Fiyo!"

"Ah, Grifo! All quiet, then?"

"Teeth and toes of the Clan-spirit, too quiet! I'm falling asleep."

"Only be careful not to let old Naucles see

you sleeping! He'll lay a thong across your shoulders to bring you out of it. He did that to me when I fell asleep the first night I was ever out on the night-herd. I've never forgotten it."

"And you've never fallen asleep on night-herd since, have you?"

Fatha laughed. "There is that, too!"

A horn sounded, far away across the herd. The two looked at each other, then kicked their horses into motion, while Fatha took up his own horn and sounded it.

They galloped around the edge of the herd, and finally came to the point where one horseman was fighting five others, using his bow and trying to avoid coming to close quarters, while still more men were trying to get some cattle up and moving.

Sounding his horn one last time, Fatha dropped it to dangle again by his thigh, then brought up his bow.

Archery by moonlight is tricky, but he managed to put two men down with three arrows, then had to drop his bow back into the case as three men bore down on him with swords.

Swordsmanship on horseback is a combination of the skilled use of the sword and the skilled use of the mount, things that any boy of the Clan learned as soon as he was old enough to be lifted onto a horse. In this sort of skirmish, it was a case of guiding the horse in close with the enemy, and using little touches of the knee to make the horse dodge away as the enemy attacked.

Fatha parried a sword-stroke from a man on his right, then struck back, a backhanded stroke which barely touched the enemy, then was forced to dodge a stroke from a man on his left. Now it was a matter of strike, parry, dodge, strike, with no time to think. With one part of his mind, he realized the raiders were driving off several cattle. There was little he could do about that, though, being thoroughly occupied with staying alive.

Suddenly there were no more enemy within reach, and the only ones he could see were riding off in the same direction as those who had driven off the cattle. Around him now were men of the Clan, including his father, and after a brief pause in which Naucles shouted out a couple of names, ordering them to stay with the herd, the rest were out in pursuit.

They could see the mass of the raiders in front of them now, slowed by the cattle they were driving off. Arrows suddenly hissed in among the pursuers, and Fatha heard his father draw in a sharp hiss of breath. The Clan were using arrows of their own now, and a moment later they were in among the raiders once more, hacking and slashing with swords.

Realizing at once that they were outnumbered, the raiders left the cattle and fled rapidly, turning in their saddles to shoot an occasional arrow to discourage pursuit. The men of the Clan turned to see to their own wounded, and drive the recovered cattle back to the main herd.

There were no few with cuts, nicks, and scratches, even one or two with arrow-wounds. Grannon had taken an arrow high in his left shoulder, and the wound was bleeding freely.

Someone suggested he dismount so they could deal with the wound properly.

"No!" he said, "Get me a wad of dry grass, and bind that around the wound with a thong until we can get back to the wagons." So they did, and he underwent the binding with clenched jaws. The ride back to the wagons could not have been comfortable, but he bore it without a word, though by the time they arrived, his face was obviously pale in the firelight.

Fatha rode beside him, ready to lend his support when it was needed. By the time they reached the wagons, the word had spread, and nearly everyone was waiting and watching for them to ride in. Fatha saw even Narolen in the back of the crowd. She wore her beaded leather cap with the beaded tassels all around, and her face went white when she saw them.

She was staring at him, and when Fatha looked down at himself, he saw that he was covered with blood, most of it his father's. He would have to reassure her about that later. At that moment, Grannon slumped out of the saddle, and Fatha barely prevented him from falling to the ground.

4. Outcast!

Grannon was dead. His wound had been serious, though none had thought it as serious as all that. He had lain in his wagon for a day, tended by his wife, Bougil and the shaman, Yopan, and the few people who looked in on him had said that he seemed to be mending.

Then, about the middle of the night, he took a turn for the worse, and by the middle of the morning he was dead.

Fatha was numb. His father, that tall, powerful man, so full of vitality, had succumbed to such a slight wound made by an arrow. There were a few who speculated that the arrow had been poisoned, for there were indeed some tribes on the Plains who envenomed their arrows, but whatever the truth of that might be, the upshot of it was that Grannon was dead.

The Clan had mourned him for three days. They had buried him, casting up a huge mound of earth over him and his weapons and goods. They had slain his favourite horse to accompany him into death, and on the top of the mound, as befit the eldest son, Fatha had poured out the horn of dark drink mixed by the shaman, while the people gathered round had cried out their woe.

There would be a further three days until the Clan chose its new leader. Barring some unusual event, that new leader would be Fatha, and he tried to bring himself to this realization. In three days it would be his responsibility to see to the welfare of the Clan; he would be the one who decided where they should go and when, he would judge disputes between Clan-members, he would be the Chieftain. And there was some part of him which filled with fear at the thought.

Many people of the Clan came to him to express their condolences, and to his stepmother. Narolen had approached, silently laid a hand on his arm, and stood by him for a few minutes, before she went away again.

So Fatha wandered in the evening among the wagons of the Wanderpeople, trying to gather his wits together, trying to prepare himself for what was to come.

A voice called, quietly. "Ah, Fatha!"

He turned. "Ah, Yopan." The shaman was old enough to have silver flecks here and there in his beard and hair, and he wore a necklace of small bones around his neck. He also wore a tight-mouthed expression, as though he were continually struggling against great agony.

"Fatha, your stepmother would like to talk to you."

"Oh?" He could think of nothing to say, save for an idle curiosity about why she would send the shaman with such a message, rather than one of the children of the Wanderpeople who were used to doing such errands. He wondered if Bougil considered the shaman to be the equivalent of a child, and only an intense effort to be courteous kept the smile off his face.

"I will go to her then." It sounded rather pompous to him, as though a visit to his stepmother was worth such a declaration. Before he could say anything else and embarrass himself further, he turned and walked back through the wagons to the one that had been his father's.

She was waiting in the wagon, seated cross-legged on the floor in the light of the flickering lamp hung on one of the struts holding up the leather cover of the wagon. When he entered, she stood up. "Welcome, son." she said, smiling.

"You asked me to come, stepmother," he answered.

She took down a skin of ale hanging on the side of the wagon, and poured some into a drinking horn, which she handed to him. "Fatha, we have not gotten along well, you and I," she said.

Fatha raised his eyebrows at that. He took the horn, thinking, 'Is she afraid I will send her back to her family? Surely I have more concern than that for what is due to my father's memory.'

Fatha took a drink as he tried to think how to answer her. He saw how she watched closely as he drank, and he saw an expression of relief come over her. He was a little surprised at that, but then she had never really known him. Even now, she had been afraid that he would refuse her hospitality, which would be a prelude to casting her back on the charity of her family.

"Stepmother," he said, "you need not be afraid. As the wife of my father, you will always have a place with my family." He drank again, to reassure her, and saw a look of triumph on her face. Surely his assurance was not worth such a display of victory?

Her eyes glittered. "You young fool! I do not need a place in your family, for you shall soon have neither place nor family. Your father did not die from his wound, you know. I had hoped he would, but it proved necessary to help nature along a little."

There was something wrong with his head. Everything was turning foggy. Bougil's words did not come through to him immediately, but he suddenly realized that she was admitting to having murdered Grannon. He stepped forward, reaching out his hands to strangle this abominable woman, but for some reason, he was moving terribly slowly.

His hands fell on her neck and he heard her scream, but the screams seemed to come from far away. Blackness closed in on him.

Suddenly he was blinking dazedly at the lights of many torches, and the faces of the people around him seemed to be full of disgust. They must have found out about Bougil as well. He heard words, but could not quite make them out. The words came again. Perhaps they were speaking to him. He shook his head to clear it.

A hand slapped his face sharply, and the voice spoke again. "Do you hear me, Fatha?" He peered closely; it was old Naucles, but he couldn't understand why they were hitting *him*.

"Yes," he said. His voice did not seem to work properly. Now it was Kofles, one of his uncles, standing in front of him, demanding answers. The words seemed to make no sense to him. His head sagged. Again, a hand slapped his face. He looked up. "Your stepmother accuses you of attempting to rape her. What have you to say to that?"

Fatha followed the words, trying to make sense of them. They were accusing him of rape?

"No!" was all he could say. There were so many words in his mind that he could not get them all out.

"You deny it, then?"

"Yes!"

"There is a witness."

Fatha heard the voice of Yopan, the shaman. "I heard screaming from inside the wagon, so I went in. I found Fatha tearing at the clothing of Bougil, who was trying to fight him off. I picked up a jug and hit him on the head with it, then we called the people together."

Now Bougil was speaking, with tears in her voice; Fatha could not yet focus his eyes on her. "Fatha came into the wagon. He had been drinking; he began to tell me that he was about to take his father's place, and that now he would take his father's place in my bed. When I objected, he began to tear at my clothes. Then Yopan came in, as he said, and struck him with a jug."

Kofles was talking to him now. "What have you to say to that?"

Fatha tried to speak now. "No, it was not like that at all. She said that she had killed my father!"

"For shame!" Yopan shouted. "Not content with attacking her, he now tells lies about her. By the Clan-spirit, if she had done something so abominable, who would be the last person to whom she would admit it?"

In his mind, Fatha had already solved that; she had wanted to have him attack her, to give more credence to the rape charge, but while he was trying to put it into words, Yopan spoke again. "And what I saw was a rape; is that what one does to a murderess?"

There was a menacing sound from the gathered people. "Cast him out!" Fatha heard.

"No!" he shouted. "Yopan, you devil!" He lunged for the shaman, but hands caught him and held him and he knew that with the effect of the drug on him, he could never break free.

"Cast him out!" Others took the shout up, and even through the drugged haze, he felt a surge of terror.

He struggled against the hands that held him, kicking out all around, trying to pull away. Something hard hit him on the back of the head, and blackness descended again.

5. Murder by Night

Fatha woke to the familiar jostle and bump of a moving wagon. His first thought was that he had had a terrible dream, but the stinging pain on his cheek soon told him it had been all too real. He sat up. But if he was outcast, who was driving the wagon? Oxen could and would go for a while without a hand at the reins, but would not likely go for very long, and from the daylight seeping into the wagon, it must have been a good many hours since---! Helpless rage came over him. Between them, Bougil and Yopan had managed to get rid of him. He wondered if any of his uncles had been a part of the plot?

But first, who was driving the wagon? He moved out to the front, finding himself still unsteady on his feet. On the wagon seat, driving the oxen, was Narolen!

"Naro? What do you do?"

She turned to look at him, and he could see the fresh cuts through her Clan-mark. "They have cast us out, Fiyo."

"Why you?"

She shrugged. "I am cast out. Let it go at that."

He sat down, silent, on the seat beside her, his shoulders slumping. He thought momentarily of taking his horse and his bow and riding back to wreak vengeance on Yopan and Bougil, even if he should die for it. But he realized immediately that it would not do. He would never get near enough to the wagons to succeed, and there was no point in being killed in a futile attempt at a futile revenge.

He remained silent, his mind full of thoughts of 'I ought to have---' 'If only I had---' and 'Why was I so stupid!' He spoke only to answer Narolen when she commented, or suggested that it was time to rest the oxen, or suggested that it was time to camp for the night. Nothing mattered very much anymore; life was over, and it was just a matter of waiting for death to come.

That night in the wagon he lay awake, staring into the darkness, wondering what he could have done, what he should have done, to make things turn out differently. His reputation among the young women of the clan had made the accusation of rape more believable. He had never forced himself on any woman, but he could see that in the eyes of the Clan, a man who enjoyed the company of women might well become a rapist.

And as for accepting a drink from Bougil, that was very careless of him. He had indeed thought that there was something wrong about the shaman carrying messages for her, but he had paid too little attention to the warning that his mind had attempted to give him.

There was someone moving outside!

Automatically, his hand dropped to his sword, slipping it out of the sheathe. He lay there for a moment, listening quietly. Yes, there was only one person outside, and that person was approaching the wagon stealthily.

Fatha moved himself slowly out of his bed; any quick movement might rock the wagon-bed, warning the lurker outside that someone inside was awake. Now, what would the person do? Most likely he would creep up to the tail of the wagon, cut loose the horse, and make off with it. While he was dealing with the horse, Fatha could leap out and cut him down.

Fatha waited patiently. The man was now outside the tail of the wagon, and Fatha hefted his sword preparatory to flinging aside the curtain and leaping out.

Then the curtain was pushed aside, and the man vaulted in, raising his sword. Fatha, his nerves keyed up, struck immediately. The man gave a kind of quiet cry and fell backward out of the wagon. Narolen was suddenly awake, sitting up in her bed. Fatha sprang out of the wagon to land beside the man, who lay in the grass. Fatha's horse was stamping around nervously, not liking the situation at all.

The man was still alive, though not for long, with that great wound in his middle. Fatha peered at the face, and with a shock he recognized Grifa. "Ah, Fiyo!" the voice was very weak.

"Ah, Grifo! What do you do here?"

Grifa gave a short laugh, which turned into a twisted grimace of pain. "I came to kill you, of course!"

"Why? What had I ever done to you?"

"Nothing, Fiyo, but she offered to pay me for the task. I am a third son, Fiyo, and if I am to make a good marriage, I must have a suitable bride-price to offer. I had little choice. And you are not part of the Clan anymore, are you?"

He gave a little gasp, then he was still.

Fatha looked up. Narolen was standing beside him. "She is not even willing to allow the customary three days. She wants you dead, Fiyo."

He nodded. "Well, she has failed. Go back to bed, Naro, while I take care of this."

"No, I will come too!"

He straightened and looked at her. "Go back to bed!"

She stood for a moment, then nodded and got back into the wagon silently.

Fatha leaned down and picked Grifo up. He was heavy, as heavy or heavier than he looked, and it was with difficulty that Fatha raised the body onto his shoulders. He staggered a little way into the darkness, then laid the corpse down.

Looking down at him, he said, "I would give you a proper burial, Grifo, but I have neither the time nor the tools. I hope that when the Clan comes up, they will find you and bury you properly."

That was, he felt, not a very secure hope.

The Clan was likely to arrive within the day, though they might well go by a mile or more from this spot. And even if they came right by this place, it was quite possible that the carrion-eaters of the Plain would have disposed of the corpse. But then, as Grifo had said, Fatha was no longer a part of the Clan, and why should he care what happened to the man who had tried to murder him?

Something occurred to him, and he made a circuit around the campsite. Sure enough, there was Grifa's horse, tethered to a low clump of brush. Fatha loosed the tether and led the horse back to the wagon. Taking off its gear, he put a halter round its neck and tethered it to the rear of the wagon beside his own horse.

He smiled grimly to himself. "So. Now I am gathering my own horse herd. I doubt I will be needing to raise a bride-price, though."

He lay awake in the wagon until almost dawn, then slept for a little while. Suddenly, Narolen was waking him up again. "If you will stir up the fire, Fiyo, I will get us something to eat before we leave."

He muttered something and sat up on his bed as Narolen went outside. He was suddenly overwhelmed with his situation again and he sat there thinking of what might have been, what should have been. Then suddenly the rear curtain of the wagon hurled back, and Narolen said crossly, "Are you going to make that fire or not?"

He realized with a start that he had been sitting there for a long time. Guiltily, he got up and went out to make the fire.

As they ate, Narolen spoke. "We had best get out of the path of the Clan. If Bougil is going to send out murderers against us, even before our three days, we ought not to make it easy for her."

He tried to think about that; the idea was a good one, but moving out of the Clan's path would simply mean that they would not be far ahead of the Clan, merely off to one side, which would make it easier for people from the Clan to find them. Perhaps it would be best to move further and faster straight forward. If the wagon broke down, however, they would be left stranded in the Clan's path, and even people who were not in the pay of Bougil might kill them out of hand when they were found.

He suddenly realized that Narolen had said something to him.

"What did you say?"

She frowned. "I asked if you were planning to answer me or not? Shall we move out of the path of the Clan?"

"Oh! Yes, we should."

6. The Water

They travelled on. Fatha found himself exhausted all the time, and he took to sleeping in the wagon while Narolen drove. She would eventually stop and, standing over him, declare that she was too tired to drive any longer and that either he must drive, or they would stay there until she was rested. He would then come out and take his turn at the reins.

On the fourth day when they rose, Narolen said, "We are out of food."

Fatha looked up at her. He was tired, even after having slept the night through, and most of the previous day, and his mind was a fog.

"One of us will have to go hunting, Fiyo. And you have more experience there than I have."

"Hunting? What's the use?"

"We either hunt, or we starve to death."

"Exactly. What use is our life now? We are without clan or family, and we will die eventually. Why make the agony longer?"

Her eyes flashed. "So Fatha son of Grannon will sit on his backside and let himself die, because his stepmother outwitted him once? How wonderful! And would not your father be proud of that?

"She fears you, you know. She fears you so much that she sent out killers before the three days, in defiance of custom. And every day that you remain alive is a victory for you. Think on that!"

Fatha felt that there should be an answer to that, but the fog in his brain prevented him from thinking clearly. Instead, he went to saddle his horse. He came back shortly with three grouse hanging at his saddle. Narolen greeted him with a smile.

Thus, the days went on. Around the endless Mother Plain they travelled, across the sea of grass, living on the wild roots that they came across, and on whatever Fatha could bring down with his bow. He still spent a good deal of his time asleep in the back of the wagon.

They came at last to the shores of a great lake. Fatha was sitting on the seat beside Narolen, trying hard to stay awake, but still constantly nodding. Suddenly she spoke.

"Fiyo, what is this lake?"

He looked up. They were travelling along the shore of a large lake, a lake so large that the further shore was only barely visible. "It is the Water, I think."

"The Water? Why do they call it that?"

"Oh, there are beings, nixies, that live in

it. But it is not considered good luck to speak of them while we are so close; they may hear us and come out to see who calls.

"I have heard that there was a time when they called it the Lake of the Goodly Ones, but even that was felt to be unsafe after a while, so now it is called only the Water."

Narolen looked out across the still silvery surface of the lake and shivered. "Well, I hope they will let us be. I think we will camp near the shore tonight. We need the water."

Fatha looked at the reeds around the shore. "And besides, there will likely be waterfowl here; we can always use more food."

They were finishing up their supper that night when there was a sound from the water. The first thing they heard was a splashing, as of a fish jumping. A little later, there was another similar splash, then there was the sound of someone wading toward them.

They looked at each other, and Fatha drew his sword, watching and waiting. Shortly, there came into the circle of firelight the figure of a naked woman.

A closer look showed that it was no ordinary woman. Her skin was greenish-white, and her hands were large, with a web of skin between the first joints of the fingers. On the sides of her neck were gill-slits, and her black hair was hanging wetly down around her back and shoulders.

She spoke to them. "What do you do here at our lake?"

"We spend the night," answered Fatha shortly.

"Oh, indeed," she answered. There was a mocking tone in her voice. "Perhaps you will spend more than the night."

Fatha put a hand to his cheek. "You see this? I am an outcast from my Clan, and that means that life and death are one to me. And that means, lady, that if you threaten us, be sure that you are willing to accept the consequences of the threat."

Her eyes widened only slightly, then she smiled a brief smile. "A threat for a threat, is it? Perhaps there is no need for threats."

"I would hope not."

"Not only heedless of death, but brief of speech as well." This time, the smile was broader. "Though on the whole, your folk and mine do not deal well together, perhaps between us, one and the other, we can deal together.

"Use the lake and its contents freely; I ask only that you be not wasteful."

Narolen drew in a sharp breath. "What sort of price do you ask for this?"

She smiled. "No, not your lives, nor the lives of your firstborn children. I fear that the old tales have not done well by us. We do not eat human children, at least, most of us do not."

Narolen was suspicious. "No price at all?"

The nixie nodded. "You do well to be distrustful of strangers. And yet I say to you that there is no price. And I will offer you as well our own help and advice."

"All this for no price? And what sort of advice would you be able to give?"

Again the smile. "No price. In times to come, when we know each other a little better, then perhaps I may wish to make a bargain with you, but what I give now is free, with no obligation to you. And as for the sort of advice, let me ask this: What is the greatest harm to come from being Outcast?"

Fatha answered this one. "We are alone, enemies to every man, prey to whoever finds us."

"And you have no allies?"

"None."

"And there is no way to find allies?"

"No." He touched his cheek. "Not with this mark on me."

"There is always a way. It only requires that one see the way when it appears."

"You are saying that there are allies for me?"

"I am saying that it is for you to find them. Does that suffice?"

"It is very vague."

She shrugged. "If the advice is good, is it not worthwhile? And where would you be if you came to depend on me so much that you could not make a decision without me?"

Fatha was suddenly aware of Narolen standing by, and was also aware that for the last while he had been saying 'I' and 'me' as though Naro did not exist. Irritation took hold on him at that moment, and he burst out, "We shall see. We shall try your advice."

"Ah, good! There may come a time in the future when we may make a bargain together."

"And your name?"

"My name? You may call me Nik-Malo."

Nik-Malo smiled again, then turned and walked back to the lake. Narolen looked after her and said, "I hope we will not regret this."

Fatha was thinking much the same thing, but he dared not admit it. "I think not," was all he said.

7. Hadar-esh

When the off-ox died, Narolen nearly broke into tears. That shocked Fatha. For up to now she had been so strong, so unwilling to give up, and he had come to depend heavily on her. Until this moment, he had not realized how strong that dependence had become.

He put a hand on her shoulder. "We will find another ox, Naro."

"Where?" She turned a fierce face toward him. "Where will we find another ox? We are doomed, Fiyo! The Clan-spirit has deserted us for certain!"

Fatha cast his eye over the countryside. It was long since he had passed this way, but he tried to remember---.

"There is a village called Hadar-esh, a day or two ahead of us. Our one ox can pull us there, and we can probably buy another."

"What do we have to buy an ox with?"

"As for that, we will see when we get there. Help me deal with the harness."

Hadar-esh was not very prepossessing. It was a collection of dwellings, small and large, on the bend of a stream. All around the village were patches of land broken up for crops, along with small herds of cattle, sheep, and goats wandering on the common grazing land.

They came down the trail toward the town and were unnoticed at first. The dogs eventually discovered them, and barked, which in turn brought several people to come to the outskirts of the town, looking at the wagon and its passengers. There were eight men in the group, each of them carrying an axe or pitchfork.

One of them, not the largest, but apparently the spokesman for the village, asked, "What do you want here?"

Like the people of Dannon-ska, these people also spoke the language of the Wanderpeople. The dialect was strong, however, and sometimes it required more than one repetition to understand them, or to be understood by them.

"One of our oxen has died, and we wish to replace it."

The group discussed the matter among themselves in low mutters, and clearly, there was some disagreement among them. Finally, the spokesman said, "How can you pay for it?"

"As to that, I will have to talk to whoever has an ox available, and when we have established a price, then I will talk about payment."

As Fatha knew, there was little money in the village, and little use for it; buying and selling was usually by barter. He hoped he could make some sort of agreement with someone to earn the ox, but that would have to be seen.

"All right. You may leave your wagon over here, on the outskirts of the village. Neither of you are to come into the village, save in the company of one of our citizens. And we will be watching you, so do not think to steal anything!"

Anger swept over Fatha, but the knowledge that they must have another ox if they were to have any chance of survival forced him to remain calm. "We will wait."

And wait, they did. They stayed there all the rest of that day, and through the night.

In the morning, Narolen approached Fatha. "They will ignore us, you know. They hope we will go away."

He shook his head. "Did you see them disagreeing among themselves when I told them we wanted to buy an ox? There is at least one of them with an ox to sell, and he hopes to make the price better by seeming unwilling."

"I hope you are right."

On that day, they were left alone again, save that children of the village came up to look at them from a safe distance. Among them was a particular boy, about thirteen years old, rather starved-looking and ill-clothed. He stayed with the crowd for a little, then someone called from the village. An expression of fear came over his face, and he ran back to the village as fast as he could. The rest stayed, and though occasionally two or three of them would tire of this amusement and drift away, others came up, and some who had gone away came back, so there was always a small crowd watching them.

In the evening, they all drifted away, leaving Fatha and Narolen alone.

They spent another quiet and solitary night. In the morning, even the children were no longer so fascinated with them, for although about ten of them came out shortly after sunup, they eventually dribbled away and did not come back.

It was the middle of the day when a man came out to them. He was stocky, thick-necked, and maintained a carefully blank expression. "You wish to buy an ox?"

"Yes," answered Fatha.

"And what have you to pay with?"

"I have my labour."

"Hm. You would earn an ox then?"

"Yes."

"How long would you work?"

"Do you buy an animal without looking at it?"

"Ah. Well, then, suppose we go look at the beast, then you can tell me how long you would be willing to work to earn it."

They went to the farmer's byre to look at the ox. In the byre was the skinny boy who had been among the other children, the one who had run in fear when his name was called. He was busy cleaning out the byre, and when the door opened to let Fatha and the farmer in, he looked up quickly, the wary look of one who has grown to expect the worst any time people approach. When he saw they were interested only in the ox, he relaxed a little, but not entirely.

The ox was not in the best of condition. It had been hard-worked, and had not been well cared-for. It clearly had a few more years of work in it, though, and Fatha was certain that if he had the care of it for a week or two, he could improve its health.

The two bargained over the ox, then. Fatha knew the farmer had an advantage in that he knew Fatha was in dire need of an ox. Fatha, however, recognized that his own advantage lay in the farmer's desire to sell the ox. He had two younger oxen, and keeping this ox would cost him in terms of fodder, a cost which he might not recoup from the labour of the animal.

They came to an agreement, six weeks' work for Fatha on the farmer's land and buildings. It was a little more than Fatha thought it was worth, but on the other hand, he did need the ox. At the end, the farmer, who gave his name as Brannon, shook Fatha's hand to seal the bargain, and Fatha agreed to start work the next morning.

8. Labourer

Fatha bent and picked up another rock and dropped it on the stoneboat. The stoneboat was a sledge consisting of a low wooden platform fastened to a pair of heavy wooden runners, hauled by an ox. The ox dragged it back and forth across the plowed field while people followed behind, picking up the stones of greater size and loading them onto it.

Once it was completely loaded, they would take it to the edge of the field and unload it.

Today, Fatha and the boy were picking up stones while Brannon worked in one of his other fields. Fatha had already discovered that the boy was named Temo, and that Brannon and his wife Gola had taken him in when he was orphaned. His status was not enviable, for though they kept him fed and clothed, he was by no means overfed, and his clothing was mostly cast-off rags that Gola had reworked into something that nearly fit him.

For all his own status as outcast from his clan and stranger to the village, Fatha could occasionally find the time to pity the boy. He wondered if Temo would eventually grow up so used to being abused that he would go through life doing work for other people and never daring to raise his eyes, or if he would some night murder the farmer and flee out to the Plains.

Of course, fleeing to the Plains would very likely only be prolonging his own death, for though the Wanderpeople lived on the Plains, and lived reasonably well, it was no easy thing for an inexperienced person to survive there.

Fatha was in good physical condition, but still the work fatigued him, and his muscles ached at the end of a day. Even then, he did not always sleep well at night, and so he was constantly tired.

Narolen was still not happy with the situation. "That farmer, Fiyo, I do not trust him."

Fatha shrugged. "Nor do I. But we have little choice in the matter. We could go on to another village with one ox, but I doubt we would find matters so much better there."

She frowned. "Be very careful, Fiyo. They dislike us, and I think they would not hesitate to cheat us, or even kill us. They probably realize that we are outcasts and that there would be no vengeance to be taken for us."

He nodded. "I know, Naro. I trust them as little as you do, or even less."

"So long as you are on your guard."

The people of the village left them quite alone, though one or two curious souls found a reason to be out in that direction from time to time. Narolen had mentioned to Fatha that men would come by to watch her while he was away. He was not sure what to do about that, and finally decided to do nothing, hoping that none of them ever went beyond looking.

One evening, after Fatha had returned from a particularly grueling day in the fields, a youngish man came by. He stood around for quite a while, then finally approached the wagon. He came up to Fatha. "A good evening to you."

"And to you," answered Fatha politely.

The man talked about the weather and the crops, but from time to time his glance would shift to Narolen. Finally he said, "She is your wife?"

"No." It occurred to Fatha that through all this time, he had never thought of Narolen as anything but a companion.

"Your sister?"

"No, my companion."

"Ah." He thought a bit, then spoke again. "What would you take to get on your horse and ride out for a little and leave me alone with her?"

For a moment, Fatha was uncertain he had heard correctly. Then he looked in the man's face and was sure that he had. His first instinct was to put his hand to his sword, but his sword was hanging in the wagon, being little more than a hindrance in the fields.

And in that moment's hesitation, he knew that giving vent to his anger here would serve only to make trouble with the villagers. He forced himself to smile. "I assume you speak out of ignorance, and therefore I will let it pass this time. But I think you had better leave now."

The man became angry, probably more from embarrassment than anything else, and seemed on the verge of saying something. All he did, however, was turn on his heel and walk away. Narolen looked at Fatha, who looked back and shrugged. "Only a few more days," he said.

9. Flight

Finally, the last day of Fatha's appointed term of labour arrived. Fatha felt uneasy; it was nothing to do with anything that anyone in the village of Hadar-esh did or said, only something that seemed to be in the air. When he went back to the wagon that night leading the ox, he was considering the situation.

Narolen looked at his face and spoke. "What is it, Fiyo?"

He shook his head. "There is no one thing I can point out, but I have a bad feeling about this town. I think it might be a good idea to harness the oxen after supper and leave."

"You think they might try to hinder us?"

"I don't know what to think. All I can say is that I have a bad feeling, and I would prefer not to be in the neighbourhood if they decide to do something."

She nodded. She walked around the cookfire, casually picking up a few things that had been taken out of the wagon during the stay, and stowed them. Then she went back to the fire. "We will have to be careful," she said. "If they are planning to stop us, they will be watching us; most likely they plan to wait until after dark, but if we begin packing up in a hurry, they will want to forestall us."

"Exactly. But if we merely pick up a thing or two from time to time and stow them in the wagon, no one will think anything of it. When it gets dark, we can harness the oxen, throw the last things into the wagon, and leave."

Dusk came. They were careful to do nothing out of the ordinary, waiting for full darkness, but with casually getting up and tossing a thing into the wagon from time to time, they were very nearly ready to go.

There was a small noise from the far side of the wagon, the side away from the town. Fatha walked round the wagon, reaching into the back as he did so to pull out his sword. Crouched a little way away from the wagon was the boy, Temo.

"What do you want here, boy?" Fatha's first thought was that Temo was part of the villagers' plan of attack, but dismissed that as ridiculous; given their attitude toward the boy, they would surely not trust him with anything important.

"I came to warn you. I heard them talking last night; they plan to come out tonight after dark and kill you. They will be coming soon. I'm sorry I couldn't come sooner; I had to wait until I could slip away without being seen."

"So why to you come to warn us? Are these not your people that you betray?"

"My people?" There was bitterness in the voice. "My people who, when my parents died, turned me over to Brannon, who is known as a cruel and harsh man? My people, who watched as he begrudged me any morsel of food, who never interfered when he beat me for the least offence, or for no other reason than that he was angry? My people, who let him treat me as one of the least valued animals of his farm? Tell me how much I owe them!"

"But I doubt if you come to warn us merely as a deed of kindness. What reward were you expecting?"

"Take me with you when you go."

"Take you with us? Boy, do you know what you ask? We are outcasts, free to be set upon and killed by any Clan or tribe of the Plains. We survive, using our wits and keeping well away from people. It is not an easy life."

Temo laughed shortly. "Tell me about the easy life I have here in the village!" he said sarcastically. "It would be a shame to throw all that away, wouldn't it?"

Fatha hesitated. "All right. Stay where you are for now, while there is still enough light that someone might see you. When we are about to leave, jump up and get into the back of the wagon as quickly as you can."

"Thank you. But don't wait too long; they will be coming soon, and your oxen cannot outrun them."

"No, that is true. But perhaps that will not be necessary. Wait there, as I said."

Narolen had come to the tail of the wagon while they spoke, seen the boy, and went back to her work. Fatha came back around the wagon and told her what he had learned.

"So we were right about them? They do not plan to let us go?"

"Apparently not. And I think we may have to take the risk of alarming them into movement; Temo says they will come soon, and as he says, it will be difficult for the oxen to outrun them. It will be impossible if the oxen are not harnessed."

"You sound as though you have a plan."

"Yes. It is rather a plan of desperation than anything else, but we may be able to make it work. After all, these villagers are not really warriors, are they? The most fighting they have ever done is to stand off a Plainsfolk raid from behind their walls. I think we can make them understand that such an attack as they plan will be costly to them, more costly than the benefit they will receive from plundering our effects."

He took three arrows out of his quiver and carefully bound a bundle of dry grass to the head of each. While he did this, he was talking to Narolen. "When I begin to saddle my horse, you take the oxen and begin to harness them. When they are harnessed, set out off to the northwest. Don't stop for me; I will catch up when I'm able."

"I hope you know what you're doing, Fiyo."

He grinned. "So do I, Naro, so do I."

He saddled his horse, and as he did so, Narolen began to harness the oxen. There was still a little light available, and in that light he could see movement in the town. Shortly, that movement resolved itself into a mob of villagers coming up the slope. Fatha vaulted into the saddle and strung his bow, then rode casually down to meet them.

Brannon was at their head, carrying a chopping axe. Fatha spoke first.

"A good evening to you, townsfolk. Where do you go?"

"You appear to be preparing to leave."

"Yes, we are. We have our ox. There is no further need to stay."

"We want to search your wagon first, to see that you have stolen nothing from us."

Fatha affected to give that some thought. "No," he said at last, "I think we cannot allow you to paw through our goods."

"You cannot allow---! How do you plan to prevent us, filthy Plains wanderer?"

There was a swell of noise from those behind Brannon, reminding Fatha of the sound of the people on the night when they had cast him out. Anger almost wiped away his plan, but he knew quite well the folly of allowing himself to come to grips with any large number of people, however inexperienced they might be as warriors. Instead of answering, he wheeled his horse and galloped back up the hill. Behind him was a shout of rage, but he knew that even the few of them who might have bows would have little chance of hitting him in that light, even if they should try.

Still, he had no time to waste. He had gained enough time for Narolen to get the oxen harnessed and the wagon rolling, but the hillslope was not enough to prevent the villagers from overtaking the wagon. He stopped by the campfire and took out one of the arrows around which he had tied the bundles of dried grass. Leaning out of the saddle, he lit the grass from the campfire. Then, holding the horse with his knees, he launched the arrow up in a high arc.

The bow of the Wanderpeople is short but strong. Made of laminated wood and horn, it can send an arrow amazingly far. Every boy of the Plains learns the use of the bow almost as soon as he is old enough to walk, and by manhood, most are experts. It was no difficult task for Fatha to launch the burning arrow towards the town, and by the time it was on the way, he was already leaning down to light the second.

Nor was it a difficult task for Fatha to estimate the range to the nearest buildings of the town, having camped in that spot for six weeks. Even though a slight misjudgement landed his first arrow in a street rather than a roof, the other two hit their targets. The villagers probably wondered why he was shooting so high, and it was not until the roof of one of the buildings was well alight they realized what he had been up to.

For most of them, the gain they might get from the goods of the Wanderpeople was not worth the thought of the destruction to be wrought in their village by fire. Eight of them, however, were sufficiently excited that they did not stop nor turn, but went after the wagon, which they could see going off into the dusk.

Fatha had hoped that the fire in the town would distract all of the townsfolk, but he was still reasonably certain that he could discourage the remaining eight. He took another arrow out of his quiver and urged his horse down towards the straggling string of people. The light was rapidly becoming worse, and shooting at any distance would be near futile. As he came, he found himself half-hoping that the man who had wished to buy Narolen would be among the eight villagers.

Shooting at the last people in the line would not be so effective as shooting at those in front, for the leaders would not see people dying behind them, though the ones coming up last might think more carefully if they saw people in front of them going down. He tried to pick out Brannon and launched an arrow. It went wide, but struck the leg of a man beside him, who fell with a cry. Fatha chose another arrow and shot again, this one being a clear miss. Suddenly, an arrow came from the back of the wagon to strike the man next to Brannon full in the chest. He went down as well.

Fatha was now past the pursuing villagers, but he turned in the saddle to launch one last arrow. It zipped past Brannon's ear to bury itself in the throat of a man behind him, and now those behind were stopping, turning, running. The big farmer turned to urge his followers on and saw that they were no longer following. He shouted ineffectual demands that they come back, shouted some equally ineffectual insults, then after turning again to shout something at Fatha, he went back himself.

Fatha was up at the wagon now and, peering inside, he saw Temo holding the bow they had taken from Grifa so long ago. "A good shot, Temo!"

"Do you think so? I was actually aiming at Brannon."

Fatha flung back his head and laughed. "Indeed? I tried to hit him several times myself. He seems to have been lucky tonight."

"Well, at least I am well free of him, and I can enjoy the thought of him getting up tomorrow to put me to work and finding that I am not there!"

Fatha went on up to the front of the wagon to tell Narolen that the pursuers were no longer pursuing. "We'd better keep going anyway, just in case," he said. "Once they get the fires out, they may be so angry that they'll want to try to track us down to get revenge. Even then, they'll probably not go too far from their town. If we go on until about midnight, then rest until morning and travel some more, we should be well beyond their range."

She looked up at him and gave him a strange smile. "Good for you, Fiyo! I was worried that we might be taking too much of a chance there, but you handled it well."

They travelled on. For a while, Fatha felt a sense of accomplishment, having successfully replaced his ox. Slowly, however, he realized all he had done was to allow them to travel for a little longer. They were still outcasts, with no actual future. The familiar weight settled on his shoulders again.

10. Travelling

They continued travelling, following the same route as the Clan was used to do, being sure to stay well out of their path. Once they saw a far off cloud of dust raised by some clan of Wanderpeople in its travels, but it proved to be easy enough to keep away from them.

They taught Temo the ways of the Plains, which gave Fatha something to do to keep his mind off his own situation. Temo did his best to learn. He was bright and capable, picking up new skills easily. But there was a little frustration in it for all concerned, for they had to teach him many things which a boy of thirteen would have known already, and many times they found that in order to teach what he had to know now, they had to compress thirteen years of training and experience into a few days.

As a result, he was never more than adequate with the bow, and though he came to be a superb horseman, the use of weapons on horseback did not come easily to him. But he learned.

One day, shortly after noon, they came over a small rise to find three cattle grazing in front of them. Fatha turned to Narolen. "Stop here for a bit. I have an idea."

He looked around carefully, then scouted the surrounding ridges. There was no sign of any owners of the cattle.

It was no unusual matter for an occasional animal or two to wander away from the herds of the Wanderpeople during the night and not be found in time to move on the next day. In fact, Fatha and Narolen had come upon such animals occasionally before. In those cases, they had usually killed the animals for the hides and the meat.

He rode back to the wagon. Narolen was looking at him as though she were trying to divine what was in his mind. "Are you going to kill them?"

"That was my first thought. I wonder, though, if it would not be better to try to drive them along with us."

"Drive them along with us? When there are only the three of us?"

"When there are the three of us, it may be more possible than it was with only the two. Look, Temo can ride well enough to take a turn at herding them, and so can I, and either or both of us can spell you at the reins. And to have cattle, even three of them, will be to our advantage when the hunting is poor."

She looked a little doubtful. "And at night?"

He pondered that for a moment. He knew what she meant; there were not enough of them to do night-herding. "At night, we can tether them to the wagon. There are only the few of them, so they will still be able to find enough grass."

She smiled then. "Good. Will you want Temo to help?"

He hesitated. Temo was still not an expert rider, and yet---. "Yes, I think so. It will give him more practice."

In the end, the cattle proved a little wild for herding from horseback. Fatha was not to be beaten, though; he chased down and caught each of them with a running loop, then dragged them back to the wagon, where he tethered them one by one to the back of the wagon on a long leather line. "They will eventually learn to follow along with us," he told Narolen and Temo. "We will keep them tied thus for a few days until they are used to living with human beings again."

Fatha was pleased with himself about the cows, though when he really thought about it, he realized he was more pleased than he had reason to be. The possession of three cows meant that successful hunting was not so vital, though it could be a matter of merely staving off starvation for a little longer.

On the other hand, the Wanderpeople always had cattle, and even a mere three cows, even without a bull to give a possibility of increase, made things that much closer to normal.

11. Encounters

They saw the great cloud of dust in front of them that signified the movement of a Clan of the Wanderpeople, so in order to avoid a confrontation, they swung out to the south. This led them up into some low wooded hills, a place where they would probably not otherwise have gone, save perhaps for wood to make repairs to the wagon.

In the middle of their second day in the area, they were poking along, with Fatha up front scouting out a trail for the wagon, and Temo handling the reins. A shadow passed overhead, and there was a sudden fierce scream, then a surprised bellow of pain and fright from one of the cows.

Fatha, turning in his saddle and bringing up his bow, saw that a griffin had dropped out of the air onto the back of a cow. He shot an arrow at it, then drew another one, noting that the beast was apparently very young; not only was it attacking domestic animals with humans about, but it had missed the killing stroke and was now trying again and again with swift stabs of its beak.

The cow, though, was moving and thrashing so much that the griffin was finding difficulty holding on to it, let alone killing it. The griffin did not seem to feel the first arrow, and at the second arrow merely twitched. At the third arrow, however, it gave a fierce bird-scream again, sprang into the air, and descended on Fatha so quickly that he almost could not get away.

He did so only by dropping from the saddle in the act of loosing another arrow. A moment later he was up, drawing his sword; the griffin, which ought by now to have abandoned the fight, sprang again like a tawny streak of lightning. Fatha's last arrow had injured a wing, so it could not take to the air, but the griffin is as quick afoot as in flight.

In this case, however, the griffin had already suffered several wounds and was a little slowed. Fatha leaped forward, ducking under the reaching paws, and thrust his sword home, then fell aside, rolling away. He came up against a sapling before he had rolled very far. If Fatha didn't move quickly, he could be trapped there when the griffin turned.

He scrambled to his feet, aware of the sandy flank of the monster as it tried to turn towards him. He was barely on his feet when it gave a last scream and fell forward. Then he saw the arrow protruding from its back, and looked back to see Temo standing at the wagon seat, bow in his hands.

"Ah, Tiyo!" Fatha called. "By the toes and teeth of the Clan-spirit, that was a good shot!"

Temo smiled in embarrassment. "Not really. "How could I miss at that range?"

Fatha grinned back at him. "Whatever the range, any shot that saves my hide, I call a good one! Now will you go see to the cow? I don't think she is injured too badly, but she may have to be killed."

Narolen got down from the wagon and walked up to stand beside Fatha. She looked at the griffin, then looked at him. "And you not even scratched?"

He looked down at himself. "No, apparently not. That must be what you call very good luck."

He stood looking down at the dead griffin. "You know," he said slowly, "I have heard it said that in some towns one can get a good price for the skin of a griffin, let alone for the beak and the claws."

She looked around. "This is not the best place to camp, though."

He looked around as well. "It could be worse. Let's stay here long enough to get this beast skinned, then we will see what we will see."

While Fatha set about his skinning, Temo came back to tell him about the cow. She was not too badly injured. Though she had several long gashes on her back and sides from the griffin's claws, and a few more around the neck from the beak, she would probably survive.

By the time Fatha got the griffin skinned, it was too late for them to travel much further, so they camped in that spot for the night. After they had eaten and about the time they were considering going to bed, Fatha noticed the horses becoming restless. He turned quietly to Narolen. "Someone or something is out there. Move back a bit out of the firelight, in case they use arrows."

Moving casually, he picked up his own bow and quiver, walking around as though to stow them in the back of the wagon. This took him well out of the light of the fire, and instead of pausing at the back of the wagon, he moved on out into the night.

Now he went extremely carefully, and quietly, stopping to listen every few steps. Whoever was stalking them was very good as well. Only infrequently did he make the least noise to betray his movements.

Fatha found a place to hide, then waited. The more he moved, the more he would reveal his own presence, and it was likely that he would frighten the stalker away to try another night. And another night, Fatha might not be so lucky.

On the other hand, the fellow would probably have noticed already that Fatha was a long time putting his bow and arrows away; how would he react to that? If he was very careful, he would be gone already.

But he was not that careful, or perhaps he was more desperate. Fatha heard the slightest shifting of leaves on a bush to his right.

Without moving more than his eyes, he looked in that direction. For a moment he saw nothing, then he saw the crouched bulk of a man about ten paces away, between him and the wagon.

Fatha raised his bow then, for some reason, he could not quite explain, lowered it. He drew his sword and came to his feet. Quickly and quietly, he came up behind the crouched figure and lay the sword on his shoulder so that he would see the gleaming blade out of the corner of his eye.

There was just enough light for Fatha to see the knife-scars on the man's cheek where the Clan-symbol would have been.

"Stand up slowly," he ordered, "And walk up to the wagon. Leave your bow where it is."

The man tensed, and Fatha knew he was going to attempt to fight. As he moved, Fatha whipped his sword back and swung. Even then, in the instant of readying his sword, Fatha decided not to kill the man, but rather slammed the flat of his blade down on his head, hard.

In the act of coming up and turning, the man crumpled and fell. Fatha moved back a little, but the man didn't stir. He watched the supine figure for a moment until he was sure that he was not shamming, then took a couple of thongs from his belt and tied the man's hands and feet. That done, he lifted the other onto his shoulder and carried him over to the fire.

Narolen watched him approach. She took things in quickly, the tied hands, the scarred face, and asked, "You did not kill him, then?"

"No. I will, though, if it proves necessary."

He dumped the man by the fire, then went back out into the darkness to retrieve his bow. By the time he had returned, the man was regaining consciousness, and seemed a little surprised to find himself still alive. Fatha sat down next to him.

"What is your name?"

"Why should you care? Kill me and have done with it."

"Had I wanted to kill you, I would have done so out there." He thrust his jaw out towards the brush. "I hope, however, that killing will not be necessary. What is your name?"

"Jochon, if it matters to you."

Fatha looked him over. Jochon was fairly large, though hard living had worn him down a bit. Jochon's hair and beard were rather carelessly trimmed and dirty. His face was naturally broad, but poor eating had thinned him so much that the bones stood out sharply. His clothing was the usual leather clothing of the Wanderpeople, though worn and tattered with age, and inexpertly patched, sometimes with patches on the patches.

"Well, Jochon, you appear to have been alone for a long while."

"A long while, yes."

"Would you like to cease being alone?"

Jochon's eyes flamed. "Don't mock me, man!"

Fatha shook his head. "No, I don't mock you. Look at me, Jochon! I bear the same mark as you. Because our clans cast us out, should we do their work for them and kill each other? Why not join together and survive?"

Jochon looked at Fatha, a look of wonderment, as though he had never thought of such a thing before.

"Join together?"

"Why not? Think of it, man! You were trying to creep up on us to take our wagon, goods, and animals, but you would find that shortly you would have to kill the cattle because you could not handle them alone. And when the wagon breaks down, as all wagons will at some time, you would be alone and unable to repair it. And eventually you would find yourself in the same situation as you are now, having gained only a year or two.

"But if you join us, then the four of us have that much better chance of survival. Three men to hunt are better than two, three men to share the herding duties are better than two. And you will share whatever goods we have as well. And perhaps we can defy those who turned us out to die and live, live longer and better than they think. What do you say to that?"

Jochon thought about that for a while, then nodded. "You are right. Set me free and I will join you; feed me some of that soup I smell, and I will be your faithful servant for life!"

Fatha grinned. "Done!" As he unfastened the thong around Jochon's wrists, he called to Narolen, "Naro, some food for our honoured guest!"

Narolen brought a bowl of soup and a spoon and handed them to Jochon. As he hungrily attacked it, heedless even of the thong still fastening his ankles together, Narolen drew Fatha aside.

"Are your serious? You will really ask him to join us?"

"Why not?"

"As well, ask the wolves to join us! He will kill us all some night and take all our goods!"

Fatha shook his head. "I think not. I think I have convinced him he would do better to come with us."

"How can you trust him, Fiyo? He is an outcast!"

"And what are we, Naro?" Her face paled, and she put a hand to her mouth. Fatha went on, gently. "You remember what the nixie said, that we should look for allies? What other allies are we going to find other than outcasts?" He put a hand on her arm and smiled. "Look, if my trust is misplaced, we lose only a year or two of life. If not, we may gain much more!"

She was quiet for a while, then she smiled a small, slightly forced smile. "All right, Fatha, I agree with you. Let us hope it works out as you plan it."

He smiled in return. "Let us hope so. And Naro?"

"Yes?"

"If you can manage it, treat him as though you trust him. I imagine it would be difficult for him to live with us for very long if you are always waiting and watching and expecting him to fail."

"I will try, Fiyo."

By this time, Jochon had finished the bowl of soup. He looked up at Narolen and said,

"My Lady, my queen, if there is another bowl of that soup, tell me what you would have me do for it? Cut off my hand? Put out my eyes? Even cut my throat, but not until I have tasted again the wonder that you perform over the cookfire!"

She snorted. "Your flattery is wasted, fellow! There is more soup. All you need do is ask for it like any normal person!"

But there was a little spark of laughter in her eyes.

Jochon proved a welcome addition to their group, for as Fatha predicted, his added hands lightened the total workload. He had a horse, a light and skittish black pony. The pony, however, had excellent manners when Jochon was riding him.

There was a little extra work at first, for Narolen insisted on making him new clothing, there being little left of his old suit. It was also necessary to produce an extension to the shelter-tent, the strip of hide which they tied slantwise to the side of the wagon to give shelter for Temo at night.

On the other hand, they had a fair bit of hide for this purpose, and it was a mere matter of cutting and sewing.

A few days later, they came upon another stray cow. This was not too surprising, given that they were so close to a clan of Plainsfolk. They brought the cow in to join their own herd, then moved off a little further away from what they thought would be the track of the clan. If cows could wander this far, it was not impossible for hunters or herdsmen to come as well, and it would not do for anyone to know that outcasts were camping nearby, particularly outcasts with cattle.

A week later, as they were eating their evening meal, Jochon suddenly looked up with a hiss of surprise. When Fatha followed his glance, he saw a small man standing in the firelight. The little man was square-built, with a slightly wide but lumpy nose. He wore garments of leather and boots of leather, and on top of it all a peaked leather cap with a bright feather in it.

Fatha was sure, from tales told over the campfires of the Wanderpeople, that this was one of the Grass-people, the little ones who were reputed to be able to work magic, and sometimes took delight in tricking human beings into difficult situations.

"A good evening to you," the little man said.

"And a good evening to you," Fatha answered. "Can we do something for you?"

"Yes, perhaps, if you are the one known as Fatha."

"I am."

"Ah. Then I must tell you this: The Kings of Endolashan and Jakashan are nervous these days. They distrust strangers within their territory, and you might be best to swing well wide of them on your travels."

Fatha looked at the little man carefully. "A useful warning, perhaps. And yet, why do you seek us out to warn us?"

The little man shrugged. "A favour for a friend. She asked me to find you and tell you this."

Fatha nodded. Nik-Malo had promised them help and advice, and was fulfilling her promise.

"Thank you, then. And when next you see your friend, thank her for me as well."

With a quick bob of the head, the little man turned away and took a step to the side. He disappeared, though there was little enough cover for him to move into. The small group of Wanderpeople looked at each other for a bit, then Fatha had to explain about the nixie. The others looked at him with a mix of awe and respect.

12. Jakashan

They continued their round of the Great Mother Plain. Jochon was continually cheerful, always addressing Narolen with an overwhelming flattery which she acknowledged only by a frown or a derisive snort. It came to be something of a game between them.

Fatha wondered occasionally how Jochon had come to be cast out, but never asked. It was better all around, he felt, if they lived as though the past was dead and gone.

They were nearing Jakashan, the city at the eastern edge of the Great Mother Plain where the river Korba flowed down from the Great Wood in the north to reach the Bright Sea in the south at the Great City Endolashan, where the King of Kings lived.

The Wanderpeople tried hard to avoid Jakashan; the King and people of Dannon-ska were thoroughly arrogant and superior, but the King and people of Jakashan were even more so. They tended to be capricious as well; where they might allow the Wanderpeople to travel freely one year, another year they would force them to pay for their passage, and another year they would forbid them to pass altogether.

And when the Wanderpeople passed, it was not unknown for people from Jakashan to harass them, and on the rare occasions when such harassment was reported to the city authorities, they laughed and drove the complainants from the city, telling them to think themselves lucky that they still had their lives.

Fatha, knowing all this, and knowing that he and his small band were even more vulnerable than the Clan of the Wanderpeople, intended to pass well to the west of the city.

By this time, they had acquired two more cows and, even more amazingly, another horse. Horses of the Wanderpeople seldom had a chance to run wild, since at night they were usually either tethered to a wagon or hobbled. It could and did happen, however. In this case, they could take the horse by surprise, and catch it with a running loop before it could escape.

It was late one afternoon when Jochon, who had been scouting ahead, rode back to report that there was another wagon on a track roughly parallel to their own, and about a half-mile ahead. "A single wagon?"

"Yes. I saw it with my own eyes, and there was no sign of any other wagon, or even of stock. Perhaps we should raid them tonight and see what they have that we could use."

"Perhaps." Yet even as he spoke, Fatha was getting another idea. "Wait, Jochon! I have an idea. Let's you and I ride over there right now!"

Jochon was a little mystified; broad daylight was not the time for making raids, and yet he accepted Fatha's orders and suggestions. He simply nodded, then waited while Fatha rode back to the wagon, where Temo was handling the reins as Narolen leaned back and watched.

"Naro, Jochon reports that there is a single wagon a little ahead of us. The two of us are going to ride over to talk to them."

Narolen was quick to understand. "You hope to convince them to join us?"

"If possible. The more we are, the safer we are."

"Be careful, Fiyo. People who are cast out are always cast out for a reason. And not all of them are going to be as willing to see reason as Jochon was."

Fatha nodded. "True. But nothing at all can be gained by not trying."

When Fatha's idea was explained to him, Jochon was even less enthusiastic about it than Narolen. He used much the same arguments, and even more forcefully. Fatha finally convinced him by promising that they would be very careful, and if the people they were approaching seemed too dangerous to be allowed to join, they would be killed. Privately, Fatha decided he would give these people every chance to prove their harmlessness, up to but not quite allowing them to loose the first arrow.

They swung wide round the wagon so as not to be seeming to creep up behind it. As they neared, Fatha could see that the wagon was very old. The hide cover had been patched in many places with a shoddy carelessness that said that the owner no longer cared for the looks of the thing. There were some parts of the wagon body which had been mended as well, and a few broken spokes in the high wheels had been mended by binding them tightly with rawhide thongs. There was a horse tethered to the back of it, a horse which seemed not to have received the best of care lately.

There were two people on the wagon seat, and they had seen the two riders at a distance. One of them, a man, held a strung bow with an arrow ready on the string. As they approached, Fatha and Jochon spread out their arms so that the two could see that they had no weapons ready. The man in the wagon raised his bow, but did not draw it. He was short and stocky, only in his forties, but he looked older. As well as the old gashes over his Clan-mark, there was another, newer, scar on the same side of his face, running from the forehead to the chin.

The woman beside him looked older than he, though she was actually younger. Her face was pinched and pale, which made the scars on her cheek show up more clearly.

When a married man was cast out of the Clan, his wife had the option of going with him and being also outcast, or staying with the Clan in the status of a widow. There were, of course, instances where both man and woman were jointly accused of a crime and cast out together.

Unless they volunteered the information, there would be no way of telling, for Fatha had determined that just as he did not ask Jochon, neither would he ask these two.

He turned his horse to ride parallel to the wagon and a little away from it. Jochon did the same, being careful to stay behind Fatha where the two could be seen, so that the man on the wagon would not think they were attempting some sort of trick.

"A good day to you."

"Is it, now?" said the man. "Be off, or I put an arrow through you."

Fatha smiled, using every bit of persuasiveness he could command, and spoke. "We come as friends. Don't be afraid."

"Friends? We have no friends. We are outcasts, even as you are, and while there is little in the wagon worth looting, still, I will do you some damage before I allow you to plunder my goods."

"But look, my friend and I are both outcasts. We are working together, and we offer you a place with us, including our help when you need help, a share of our goods and the products of our hunting, and our aid when defence is needed."

"Fine talk. What help can you be, with two men, two horses, and no sort of equipment?"

"Our equipment is back with our wagon. If you look back, you can see the cloud of dust it makes."

The man looked, and alarm came to his face, then was cleared away quickly. "That is more dust than could be made by a single wagon!"

Fatha nodded. "Quite right. We have a few cattle as well."

"Cattle? How does an outcast come to have cattle?"

"By rounding up the strays that we come across. We have very few, but with more people to help in the herding, we might be able to handle more."

The man glanced quickly at the woman, who looked up at him, then the man said. "Very well. Bring up your wagon to join us, and we will see how we feel. How many are you?"

"There are myself, Jochon here, my companion Narolen, and a boy named Temo from the village of Hadar-esh."

"So. Be careful, then. We will travel together for a while, but if you have attempted to deceive us, woe to you."

"Fair enough. You will find that we have not deceived you. What are your names?"

"I am Moshna, and my wife is Sarinen. And while you have told us the names of all your party, you have not named yourself."

"Ah!" Fatha smiled and felt himself flushing a little. "My name is Fatha."

Fatha and Jochon rode back to their wagon and brought it and the stock up to join with Moshna. When they returned to Moshna's wagon, they saw he had neglected to inform them about something; there were three children in the wagon, two boys of about five and six years and a girl about twelve.

He pointed to them in order of age. "These are Jashil, Konja, and Vrannon. They stay back in the wagon when we meet with strangers." It was said in a manner which showed that this was as much of an apology as they were likely to receive for being misled.

Fatha merely acknowledged the introductions.

Three days later, Jochon, once more scouting ahead, rode back swiftly to report the approach of a troop of heavy cavalry. "Ten of them, Fatha, out of Jakashan, bows, arrows, lances, swords, scale armour and helmets. If they decide to attack us, we cannot fight them. Perhaps we should move a little further west?"

Fatha shook his head. "We are making sufficient dust. They will have already noted our presence, and we cannot move fast enough to escape from horsemen. And if we try, they will likely only become suspicious and who knows what that will lead to?"

He rode over to inform Moshna, who frowned at the news. "I do not like this, Fatha. What do you plan to do?"

"Do? With three of us against ten heavy cavalry? We will be extremely polite and hope that they will pass us by with only a glance. It is our only hope, Moshna; we dare not fight unless there is no other alternative."

The older man nodded. "Keep our bows strung, but in the case?"

"Exactly."

The soldiers came riding up shortly after that. The Captain was prideful and arrogant, and he viewed the people and wagons with suspicion. Fatha had ridden forth to meet him.

"What do here?" he demanded. The language of Jakashan, unlike that of Dannon-ska, was not related to that of the Wanderpeople, and though certain of the people of the city learned enough of the language to get by, they did not consider it important enough to speak properly.

"We only pass through, honourable Captain."

"Pass through? This land belong Jakashan. You know?"

"We are aware of that, honourable Captain. We do not stop, we do not stay, we only pass through."

"You pay for passage?"

"We have little to pay with, honourable Captain."

"Ha! We see. You not rich, for sure!" He laughed at that witticism, and Fatha, after the Captain gave him a sharp glance, laughed as well.

The Captain surveyed the wagons and the stock, then turned and barked an order to one of his men. It was in his own language, so Fatha did not understand until the Captain turned and spoke to him. "We take one of your cattle."

"But honourable Captain, we have only a few cattle!"

The Captain smiled at the protest. "You not wish to pay for passage?"

"Oh yes, honourable Captain. Only---"

"Then we take fee. One of your cattle."

Fatha considered whether or not to argue more. If he did not argue at all, the Captain would likely think that he had let them off too easy, and demand more. On the other hand, arguing too much would merely anger the Captain, who would then be likely to retaliate. He said, "So be it, honourable Captain."

He was reminded again of the day that he and his father had talked to the King of Dannon-ska. And he remembered his father's reaction to the notion of attacking the city: Better to put up with petty harassment than to fight a battle which would only cost them losses they could not afford.

The soldiers picked, of course, the best of the cattle and killed it there and then. Fatha was back beside Moshna, urging him in a low voice to stay still and do nothing.

"It is our choice, Moshna. We either let them do what they will or we die, and then they do what they will anyhow. Stand quiet, let them be, and with luck, they will let us go." It was a tense moment before Moshna relaxed and let his bow slip back into the case again.

"I do not like it, Fatha!"

"I like it even less. But we must stay alive."

The Captain rode over to Fatha. Fatha could tell that the Captain was pulled two ways; he wanted on the one hand to bait the Plainsfolk into a fight in which he could justifiably kill them all, but he was just a little concerned that such a fight could possibly cost them one or two casualties, which would have to be explained to his superiors.

"Why you wait here? Go!"

"Yes, honourable Captain."

Fatha led his people on along their way. But he told himself that somehow, sometime, he would find a way to pay back the City of Jakashan.

13. The Bright Sea

Five days later, they added to their band again. This time it was a young man alone driving a fairly new wagon, with the marks of the outcast fresh on his cheek. He was angry, hurt, mistrustful, and a little wild, but he could see the benefits of belonging to a larger band. His name was Chogu, and he was an excellent bowman.

He was also somewhat skilled in the making of wheels, a fact they discovered when Moshna's off rear wheel finally broke down completely. After the men surveyed the splintered wreckage, it was decided that they should put a temporary skid under that corner of the wagon until they could find a town where they might buy a new wheel.

Chogu spoke up then and said, "Why not build a new wheel instead?"

"Do you know how?" Fatha asked. "None of us have that ability."

"I am not an expert, but my father was, and I learned a few things from him." His face tightened as unwelcome memories returned.

"So! Tell us what we will need, then!"

So Chogu listed the things they would need to build a new wheel, chief among them being the proper wood. "It would be best to have the wood cut, dried, and seasoned before we built the wheel. That may not be possible. Of course, we could cut the wood and let it dry and season while we travel, and in the meantime we could build an emergency wheel to make do."

They found a stand of wood within a couple of days' travel and, under the direction of Chogu, they cut the wood they needed.

They were still travelling with a skid under one corner of Moshna's wagon when they came upon the caravan, a trader with a string of laden camels and ten men guarding it.

Jandarth the trader was a wizened and swarthy man, with very bowed legs. He did not entirely trust the Wanderpeople, but considering that there were so few of them, he was willing to at least greet them in a friendly fashion.

He exchanged greetings with Fatha, and just as they were about to say farewell, it occurred to Fatha that this might be just the opportunity to sell the griffin hide that was in his wagon.

"Trader, would you be in the market for a good hide?"

"Hide?" Jandarth frowned. "There is a market for hides, but I myself do not trade in cowhide. A single hide, or even several, would not be worth my while. Perhaps a wagonload, but even then---" He let the sentence trail off in a discouraging fashion.

"Ah, but I was not speaking of cowhide."

"What, then?"

"What would you say to the hide of a griffin?"

Jandarth betrayed nothing in his face or voice. "A griffin? For certain? Believe me, man, you cannot do with me as you might with some and pass the skin of a lion off as that of a better beast."

"Oh, most definitely a griffin."

"I would have to see it first."

"Of course."

So the two groups paused, and Fatha dickered with the merchant over the skin. Jandarth frowned at the skin and said that it was a very young beast, clearly. It would not be worth very much. Fatha was silent.

"I will give you fifty silver pieces for it."

Fatha laughed. "For fifty silver pieces, I will cut it up and use it to tie my wagon together. A hundred gold."

"O Plainsman, you are dealing with a merchant, not with the King of Kings. Ten gold."

"O merchant, you are not dealing with a total fool. Ninety gold."

So the bargaining went, with the merchant pointing out such things as the several arrow holes and cuts made by the sword, and

Fatha pointing out that it was nevertheless a real griffin skin. The end of the deal was that he sold the skin, the beak, and the claws to Jandarth for a total of seventy-five gold pieces.

It was more gold than most of the outcasts had ever seen at one time. They had had little use for gold, for in the Clans things were traded back and forth, but money practically never used. For the things they occasionally bought from the villagers, they usually paid in goods, hides and the like. The gold that Fatha's Clan had paid to the King of Dannon-ska had to be laboriously gathered by selling things to the towns along their route.

A few days later, they actually spent a little of the money in order to have one of their cows bred to a bull in a village along their way.

The Wanderpeople always swung well inland to avoid Endolashan, the city of the King of Kings. The outcast band, being even smaller and more vulnerable, went even further inland, moving gradually further south until they were within eyesight of the Bright Sea.

As they camped on one of their sites near the Bright Sea, late in the evening when all had eaten and they were sitting around the fire telling stories and singing songs, Nik-Malo walked into the light of the fire.

"Ah, Fatha!" she said.

"Ah, Nik-Malo! This is not your lake!"

She laughed. "No, indeed! But I may go wherever water goes, you know. And so I chose to come down to the Bright Sea to visit you here."

"You are welcome among us, Nik-Malo."

She laughed again. "Look at your people before you say that, Fatha. Some are afraid of me, some are wondering whether they could manage to put an arrow through me quicker than I could put a spell on them! But I assure you, I have not come to do you harm."

Fatha looked around at his people, and saw that all of them were indeed apprehensive, and that some hands were creeping toward weapons. "Stop!" he shouted. "This is Nik-Malo, a water-spirit, and she is friendly. Leave your weapons be; she will not harm us!"

It was clear that not all of them trusted Nik-Malo even with his assurances, but they had all become used to treating him as a chief and trusting his judgement. They sat quietly and waited.

The nixie spoke again to Fatha. "I see that you have found some allies. I applaud you. But you must think ahead as well. Consider what certain people will think when they hear of a gathering of outcasts. You will have to be ready to defend yourselves. The problem is that you need to add members to your band in order to be safe, but the more members you add, the greater will be the danger of being attacked."

"You have a suggestion for me?"

"No, I will not do all your thinking for you. I merely give you warning, and leave the response to you. If you depend too much on me to tell you what to do, will you not be more likely to lead your people to a disaster because I could not be there to advise you all the time?"

Fatha bowed his head in acknowledgement. "I thank you for the warning, Nik-Malo."

"You are welcome. But there is one other thing. I need your help with another thing. It may be dangerous. I will not hide that, though I hope that the danger will not be great."

Fatha's mind was telling the tales of the campfires of the Wanderpeople, how such beings as this would make bargains with men, bargains which brought tragedy and disaster.

She smiled, as though she read his thoughts. "You fear me? Perhaps you do well to fear that which you do not know. Yet I swear to you that I have no ill-will toward you, and that I have no wish to see you harmed. I need only your assistance in this matter."

He looked up at her and made up his mind suddenly. "I will do it."

"Good! There is something I wish you to keep for me until the time when I need it again. Can you do that?"

"I can keep it," said Fatha slowly, "but what will I need to guard it against?"

"Probably against nothing. It may never even be discovered that you have it. But never fear, if anything should approach which is beyond your ability to fight, you shall have my help."

He nodded. "So, then. What is this thing that I must guard?"

She put her hands together and blew into them lightly, then drawing her hands apart, she displayed a small round clear stone attached to a golden chain. She reached forward and hung it round his neck.

"Keep it until I ask for it again," she said.

"I will." She was smiling at him.

"Yes, I know you will. Farewell, then, Fatha." She turned and walked back into the night.

14. Skirmish

As they travelled, Fatha considered all that the water-sprite had told them. It was clear to most people, a gathering of outcasts would present a danger. The Wanderpeople would consider all these to be wild, Clanless folk, likely to attack any Clan at any time, for any reason or for none at all. To the cities, towns, and villages, they would be people who had been cast out by the Wanderpeople, and must therefore be even more vicious and barbarous than those who had cast them out. And if many of these were gathered together, what might they do to civilized folk?

As Nik-Malo had said, however, they were in a trap. In order to have any safety against attack, or even against natural disaster, they had to recruit more members. The more members they recruited, the more of a danger they would appear to the people around them.

At present, it was unlikely that many knew the existence of a band of outcasts. News would spread, however, and eventually everyone would know of them. When that happened, they would be in serious danger.

There were too few of them to fight the way the Wanderpeople were used to, swirling masses of horsemen loosing clouds of arrows, closing in for a couple of strokes of the sword, then riding away again.

Fatha finally reached a conclusion; there was one way at least in which they might fight and have some hope of survival. He explained it first to Jochon.

"What! Crouch behind wagon-boxes to fight? That is not a man's way!"

"Jochon, if we were several hundred strong, I would agree with you. We are not. We have a few men with us, some children and some women. A party of ten heavy cavalry from Jakashan could destroy us in two minutes of fighting in the open, and after that the women and children would be at their mercy. Even this way, we will be in severe danger, but at least we have a small chance of survival."

"I do not like it!"

"No more do I, but we will do it, and we will survive."

They began practicing to swing their wagons into a circle, unhitching the oxen and moving them inside the circle, then joining the wagons nose to tail, with the yoke pole of one thrust underneath the one in front.

They also took to sending scouts out far forward and to the rear, so that the band might be warned early in case of danger.

As they moved westward, they picked up two more outcast families. In one family, as well as the man and wife and five small children, there was a boy on the edge of manhood who could handle bow and sword, a welcome addition to their fighting strength.

That fighting strength was needed shortly. They had been travelling for only a little while one morning when Temo came riding up rapidly from the rear. "Fatha! There is a patrol of soldiers coming up behind us."

"What sort?"

"Heavy cavalry. Ten of them. They were riding along the Shore Road from Endolashan, but they appear to have turned off to follow us."

"Good work, Temo." Fatha considered for a moment sending the boy out to try to find Moshna, who was scouting forward today, but rejected the notion. He might not be easy to find, and it would then entail being two fighting men short rather than only one. "Pass the word to the rest that we will prepare for them on that little knoll up there, then you get back and watch the soldiers. Try not to let them see you, and certainly do not let them catch up to you before you get back."

The men on this patrol were all wearing iron helmets and coats of leather with iron scales sewn on them in an overlapping pattern. They carried shields, spears, and swords, with bows and arrows cased at their saddles, much as the Wanderpeople did. Their Captain was a thin man, somewhat old, and his mouth seemed continually set in a thin angry line. He sent a single man up toward the ring of wagons to talk to the people there.

"Who are you, and what are you doing here?"

"We are Wanderpeople," Fatha answered, "and we are passing through."

"Have you paid for your passage?"

"We have nothing to pay with."

"We will search your wagons."

Fatha considered this. If he rejected the demand to search the wagons, there would certainly be a fight. If he allowed the soldiers to search, they would certainly lose gear which they could ill afford to spare. "We have nothing in our wagons but the usual tools, beds, and such."

"We will see."

"We would prefer that you do not try."

"Either we search them as you watch, or we search them after you have died. It does not matter to us."

"But will it matter to you if you die trying? We will not allow ourselves tamely to be killed."

"I go back to take your words to my Captain. I would suggest that you move your wagons apart and prepare to be searched."

Fatha said nothing, but watched the other turn and ride away. He himself rode back into the circle of wagons and watched the soldiers. The soldiers, in turn, waited and watched as well.

Finally, satisfied that the people behind the wagons were not going to come out, the soldiers thrust their lances into the turf, took out their bows, and rode up the slope. Fatha decided to let them come as close as possible before ordering his people to shoot; the soldiers were armoured, so an arrow would have to strike them squarely in order to penetrate.

The soldiers had a disadvantage, however; they would be shooting uphill, which made it more difficult to judge one's aim. Suddenly, they let loose a flight of arrows.

Most of those arrows struck the wagons, though some of them buried themselves in the ground inside. It would allow the soldiers to have some idea of how to aim, however. Fatha called out, "Loose arrows!"

Arrows lofted from behind the wagons, and suddenly two soldiers were down. But the soldiers were not to be stopped easily; they urged their horses to move faster, then up the hill they came. Arrows were flying both ways now, and more soldiers were down.

But not all the losses were on the part of the soldiers. As he shot, Fatha could see that one of his people was down with an arrow in him, and that Chogu was still shooting despite an arrow through his thigh.

The impetus of their charge brought the soldiers up almost near enough to touch the wagons, but by then half their number were gone, including the captain. Two more tumbled from their saddles, then the last three turned and rode away. Fatha jumped for his horse. "After them, quickly! If they escape to bring more soldiers after us, we are dead!"

He was away, without looking back to see who, if anyone, was following him. The soldiers had gained some distance while he was getting his horse out from inside the wagons, but the soldiers' horses were not fresh, and they were carrying men wearing armour. Fatha shortly made up the distance.

At what was rather far range for his bow, he let loose an arrow. It skimmed by a little to the side of one of the soldiers, but encouraged them all to bend double over their horses' backs. He took up his reins again and urged his horse to greater speed.

He caught a glimpse of something black out of the corner of his eye, and there was Jochon galloping up beside him. They were coming closer now; one soldier straightened in his saddle, then turned right around to loose an arrow at Fatha. Fatha buried his head in his horse's mane, and the arrow went by overhead. He straightened, preparing his own arrow, only to see that soldier falling from the saddle with an arrow in his back.

Fatha aimed at one of the other two, shot, missed, then shot again and hit. The last soldier pulled up his mount, swung the animal in a circle, and came charging back towards the Plainsfolk, drawing his sword. He dropped with one of Jochon's arrows in his chest before he had come more than a few yards.

Fatha pulled up his horse, and Jochon brought his own horse dancing around in a circle to stand beside Fatha. "Now what?"

"We round up the horses," Fatha said, "and we take from the bodies anything which can be useful to us. And we prepare to march as soon as possible."

"The horses, the armour, they will all be recognizable. The horses wear the brand of

Endolashan, and the armour is of the sort issued to the cavalry of Endolashan."

"We will sell the armour and most of the weapons in the larger towns around Dannon-ska. They may recognize where they come from, but they will not likely care. As for the horses, while I would like to keep them with us, I fear that they too must be traded away. With any luck, we can trade them for some less-recognizable animals."

15. Retaliation

The victory had not been without cost; three men and two women had been wounded, one woman severely, and one man was dead. This was serious news for a band so small as the one that Fatha led, and he spent some time considering ways and means of limiting such losses in the future.

The town of Glanta-esh was a large town, situated on the caravan route north from the western end of the Bright Sea to Dannon-ska. It was large enough to support a merchant who made his living in buying and selling of whatever came his way. The merchant was willing to buy the armour, though he pointed out that the fact that it belonged to the King of Kings in Endolashan meant that it would have to be taken apart and used as scrap metal, and this would affect the price.

And as for the horses, they would not be saleable to the east, which would also affect their prices.

On the other hand, as Fatha pointed out, the horses were fine horses, and if he sold them to anyone who had no plans to travel to the East, he could get a good price for them himself. And if the bargain was too steep, then Fatha would take his horses and go, trusting in his own ability to prevent their presence from becoming known in the territory of Endolashan.

The end result was that Fatha came away with some supplies that they needed quite badly, along with four new horses and two new oxen.

Just outside the village of Glanta-esh, they picked up a new family. The cuts which defaced the Clan-marks were still fresh on their cheeks, and they were bitter and angry with their lot. That being so, they were not readily convinced of the safety of numbers. In the end, though, they joined the band.

One thing the band could not do yet was to mount a night-herd sufficient to deter raiders. They kept a couple of people out to keep off four-footed predators, but one night a band of men ran off practically all their stock. It was a shock to them, and many of the band, who had thought themselves fairly safe, now began to wonder.

Fatha called Jochon to him. "They left a track?"

"Yes, but if you are thinking of raiding to bring our cattle back, we do not have the men."

"We have, if we use them properly. Ask the people to gather."

Fatha sat up on the front of his wagon and the people gathered around him. Most of them were curious, wondering what he was proposing to do. Some were still angry at what had happened, and some were frankly fearful.

"Well, we have lost our cattle. We can accept that, accept that being outcasts, we have no rights, no alliances with larger clans to retaliate, or we can retaliate by ourselves."

"Retaliate?" Moshna was frowning. "By the tracks of the raiders, there were twenty warriors in the party, which probably means upwards of fifty warriors in the Clan from which they came. And we will retaliate?"

"I have a plan, Moshna, a plan which would permit us the luxury of retaliation, without undue risk. Provided, of course, that we are not too greedy."

Thus it came about that Fatha and a few others sat in the lee of a hill waiting in the cool of the night for the planned raid to begin.

They required a diversion. Fatha had already arranged that, and all it needed was for Temo and the man with him to begin their work. Unless they had been found and caught by some wide-ranging scout, a remote possibility, but still a possibility. The men were becoming a little restless, and Fatha was not sure how much longer he could hold them here. Most of them were probably thinking the same thing; if the two had been discovered, would that not start the warriors of the Clan searching for whoever else might be skulking around? In which case, Fatha and his party were in severe danger.

He wondered if he had not better call the whole thing off. In that case, though, he would have to send someone, or go himself, to find the other two. In the dark, that would not be easy to do. If they were merely taking a little time getting into position, and began the diversion as he was searching, then they would be all alone with no support.

And yet, risk the two or risk them all? Which could he choose?

Moshna let out a sigh. "There!"

Fatha and the others looked; a small spark of light showed in the sky, then plunged down. Another followed it, and another, and another. The men looked at Fatha, waiting for the command.

"Not just yet. Give them a little time to become thoroughly upset and confused about it. Then we go!"

He held them there, held them even a little longer than he thought was necessary because it seemed to him that his mind kept telling him to hurry. "Now!"

In a galloping mob, they went up over the hill, whooping down toward the herd of cattle below. Off in the distance, they could see fires among the wagons, even some wagons blazing. Temo and his companion had done well at dropping burning arrows into the camp; one or two wagons burning was a serious matter for the clan, and a good deal of their attention would be on those. There would also be warriors out looking for the people shooting the burning arrows.

He hoped the two had not stayed around too long; it would be no brilliant victory to take cattle from the Clan at the expense of two lives that they could ill afford to lose.

The cattle, already made nervous, were startled into movement. The night-herders, caught by surprise, sounded their horns and rode over to meet the raiders.

But now that the cattle were going, the raiders, rather than trying to cut out a few and take them away, gave a few more yells to keep the cattle moving, and rode back up over the hill.

The cattle would run for quite a while, Fatha knew, and it would be difficult for the night-herders to bring them under control, though they would eventually do so, especially with the help coming from the camp.

Once over the hill, Fatha looked at his little band. "You all know your tasks. Go!"

Several of them immediately went off in the general direction that the cattle had taken, while he and a few others went down toward the camp. Along the way, each of them took the one or two extra horses he had tethered nearby.

Paradoxically, because of the great alarm in the camp, it was easy to approach. Several warriors were out combing the hills and coulees for the people who had launched the fire-arrows, a few others were out trying to stop the stampeding cattle, and the rest were busily trying to control the fires in the camp.

This part of the plan was the most dangerous, though, and the most likely to prove fatal to the outcasts. Fatha had impressed upon them the necessity of being careful, but even so, it was dangerous.

The first thing he did was tether his horses outside the camp. Next, he crept up on his stomach to a point where he could survey the camp and see what he had to see. There were a number of children watching the fire from a safe distance, with several women watching over the children. He could hardly have hoped for better!

He got up and walked swiftly into the camp, walking as though he had every right to be there. He approached one woman, who looked up at him. Her eyes widened as she realized he was no member of the Clan. He already had a dagger out, and he stepped to her side, holding it close to her. "If you try to give an alarm, you will die, and you will die before anyone can help you."

"What do you want?"

"Come with me?"

"With an outcast? Never!"

"Not so loud, or you die. Don't worry, I have no desire for a wife. I only need your presence for a while."

She still hesitated; he pricked her side a little with the dagger, and she started, then moved. As they went, he held the dagger close to her side.

Nobody seemed to pay any heed to their departure. When they were outside the camp, he led her to the horses. She was still quiet, but he knew that shortly her fear of the knife would be less than her fear of being the captive of an outcast.

He put the knife away, whipped out a scarf, and tied it round her face, then tossed her into the saddle, quickly tying her legs under the horse's belly to prevent her from throwing herself down while they rode.

He leaped into his own saddle and led her away, urging the horses into a run. He saw she was already trying to remove the scarf, but by the time she succeeded, her shouting would do little good.

16. Murder and Punishment

They marched the next day, with scouts out and wary. A little before noon, a scout reported the approach of numerous mounted warriors. Fatha mounted and rode out to speak to them.

He did not ride far, for his status as outcast meant that anyone who saw him could kill him, and he needed to speak to the warriors before they did anything. He stayed close to the wagons and waited as the warriors rode up.

The leader of the party was a stocky little man, wizened and grizzled, and no fool. He spoke to Fatha brusquely. "Outcast! You have our cattle."

"Yes, but then you took ours. We are even."

"Not quite. You have some of our women as well."

"We have, and we keep them as surety against you. If we are let to go unhindered, we will let them go."

"And if we kill you and take them?"

"Then they die before any of us, and we then see how many of you we can kill."

The chief thought that over a little, then said, "Even if we do allow you to go, what guarantee do we have that you will release our women?"

"You have our promise."

"A promise given by renegade outcasts! What is that worth?"

Fatha felt the anger growing in him, but he pushed it back. "You have two choices, O chieftain. You can let us go, and trust that our promise is good, or you can kill the women we have with us by attacking. But ask yourself, what will the husbands of the women say when they know that you might have saved them?"

He spoke loudly enough for all the men behind the chief to hear, and was gratified to hear in response a little mutter running through the group.

"So. We let you go, then." The chief made no threats or promises of what would happen in the future should their paths cross, but Fatha knew that all these things were in his mind.

"Good. Now, listen to me, and listen carefully. We will travel on this day, and we will be looking behind us. If we see the dust of your wagons and herds moving behind us, we begin killing the prisoners. And do not think that you will be able to rest today and travel by night, for we will have scouts out. If you appear not to have broken faith, then we will release the first of them tomorrow morning. By the third day from now, if all is well, we will have released all of them. Agreed?"

"Agreed," the Chief muttered. He was not happy about the agreement, nor the manner in which it had been forced on him.

The outcasts' wagons rolled on. They kept careful watch, but the chief could apparently control his clan, and there was no pursuit.

The outcome of the situation did not entirely satisfy Fatha; the killing of women had always been frowned upon among the Wanderpeople, and yet, what choice had they? They had had to recover their cattle or face eventual death, and they had had to work with what they had. They were too few yet to mount the normal sort of return cattle-raid, too few to fight against a determined attack by any but the smallest of clans.

He wondered if he would really have killed the women, then decided that he probably would have, though he would not have liked to do so.

As for the cows, they had not exactly recovered the precise cows they had lost, but they had taken from the other Clan's herd approximately the same number as they had lost.

They went well south of Dannon-ska; though the grazing was poorer, there were less likely to be patrols of soldiers from the city. In this area they came upon another group of outcasts, three families of them, who had banded together much as the group under Fatha. The three gladly joined the larger group, which was gradually assuming a size which rendered it less vulnerable to raids and attacks from others.

But on the other hand, there were troubles. Two young men sought the favour of the same young woman, and one of them, his emotions getting the better of his good sense, crept up on his rival in the night and stabbed him dead.

He was, of course, the first one to be suspected, and although he tried to deny the crime, they found blood on the sheathe of his dagger where the weapon had been put away without being cleaned properly. They brought him before Fatha to be judged.

Fatha heard the tale and the evidence and looked at the young man. "This is true, Goma?"

Goma, having been caught once lying, could think of nothing to tell but the truth.

"It is."

"Why?"

The night before, in all his madness, Goma had seen murder as the only solution to his problem, as something justified and understandable. This morning, standing before family and friends, and the relatives of the dead man, it all seemed foolish madness, and though he tried to speak three times, all he managed to say at last was, "I must have been mad."

Fatha frowned. "We are all outcasts. There is little more that we can do to a man who takes the life of his comrade, for casting out from such a group as ours means little. Therefore, I say that the punishment for this will be death."

Somewhere on the outskirts of the crowd, Fatha heard an anguished girl's voice cry out, "Giyo!"

There was silence. Fatha looked around at the assembled people. "We cannot afford quarrels or troubles among us. We are still too few, so few that an accident could destroy us by a night's raid. Nor can we afford to lose two men because one man kills another.

"Goma, you are condemned, and the manner of your death shall be this: When the day comes that a man is required to die to hold back pursuit, or a man is required to undertake dreadful danger for the sake of the people, that will be your task."

Fatha looked around at the people. "There are some who may not be happy with this sentence, some who would prefer to see this man die now, or be driven out. Remember, as you think this, that we have too few people to waste lives heedlessly. And if your anger burns in you, remember that it is 1my0 decision, and that who would contravene my decision must answer to me."

He could see that there were those in the crowd who were still not completely satisfied, but he hoped they would at least remain patient.

He thought about Goma for much of the day, when he was not concerned with all the other difficulties and problems of leading a group of Wanderpeople. Goma and his victim had desired the same woman; he wondered if they had considered at all the difficulties of wedding and fathering children without a Clan. But then, as he remembered, thought had very seldom played a part in that sort of thing.

And that turned his mind to Narolen. For all this time, a year or more, they had been sharing the same wagon as companions, and yet he had never considered trying to be more to her than a companion. He wondered about that, too, and wondered where his wits had been. Of course, she had seemed quite content with the situation, and gave no sign of wanting to change their status.

That night, as they were preparing the beds in the wagon, he took her by the arm and turned her around. "Naro," he said, then could not think what to say next.

She smiled at him. "Not yet, Fiyo."

"Not yet?" He felt a sinking feeling in his stomach.

"No. But I will tell you when."

He smiled. "Ah. Not yet, but sometime."

"Sometime," she agreed. She looked for a moment as though she would say more, but she shook her head briefly, then turned away to her own bed.

17. Duinifaire

The journey continued. Around the Great Mother Plain they went, carefully scanning the horizon for the dust-plumes that would signify other clans on the move, and always trying to remain at a distance from them. Their increased numbers made more noise on the march, and they were therefore no longer finding so many stray cows. Fatha took to sending out scouts specifically to look for cattle, and by this means, they continued to build up their herd.

Some outcasts, particularly those who had been wandering the plains alone for more than a year, had given up the careful attention to the state of their wagons, which had been their habit when they still lived with their Clans. Within a Clan, of course, the mere unspoken disapproval of one's companions was enough to stir all but the very laziest to take some pride in the appearance of their wagons.

As an outcast, usually with no pride left at all, there was often little or no incentive to do anything save the most basic repairs, which kept the wheels turning and the cover from leaking. Now that they were back in a group again, most of them began to show more concern for their equipment, though some few had let things slip to a point where they felt that little could be done.

At first Fatha had considered dropping a word quietly in the ear of each of these, but before he did so, he thought the situation over again. Their wagons were in such a state that they were barely repairable, and their owners probably saw the job as being beyond their own capabilities. To let them know for certain what they probably already suspected, that everyone else had noticed the state of their equipment, would only make matters worse.

In the end, he picked out some men whom he knew could be depended on to handle the matter properly, and had one of them approach each of the men in question with a suggestion that the two of them get together and fix one specific thing about the wagon. In most cases, other men, seeing them working on the wagon, went to help out. The job, which was too much for one pair of hands, was rather easier when undertaken by several.

There were wagons among them, though, which were on the point of complete breakdown. Even the toughest wood and leather can last only so long, travelling through wind, rain and sun. Eventually repairs are impossible.

There were two fundamental ways of getting new wagons: building them for oneself, or buying them from among the towns and villages. Building one required a large investment in manpower and materials, buying one was extremely expensive. The villagers disliked the Plainsfolk and did their best to drive a hard bargain.

As for building a wagon, that involved getting the material, either lumber previously cut and aged, or cutting it and aging it oneself. For ready-cut lumber, one could approach the towns and villages, and again the matter of expense came in. After consultation with his people, Fatha decided it would be best if they cut their own lumber.

They marched northward, toward the Great Wood.

About the middle of the third morning of their march north, they came upon a strange sight. As they came over a hill and moved downward, they saw in the middle of the trail a small man, one of the Grass-people, fixing his wagon.

The wagon was small, as suited the size of the small brown person, and so were the two oxen tethered nearby. The wagon had suffered a broken rear axle, which meant that in order to do the repairs, the rear corner of the wagon had had to be lifted off the ground. He had achieved this by means of a long pole braced over a large block of wood. Tied to the end of the pole were several baskets, each of them filled with stones. As the little man had increased the weight of stones, the pole had gone down and eventually the wagon had gone up.

This had not been the work of a couple of minutes, of course. The small man must have been there for some hours. What had happened to the scouts? Why had they not seen him?

Even as he considered this, Fatha remembered that the tales of the Little Brown Ones, the Grass-people, said that they were seen only when they wanted to be seen. He suddenly shivered as he realized what that meant! Why would this person want to be seen by Fatha's band?

The little person looked up as the band moved down the slope. Casually, he went to the front of the wagon and took out a bow and arrows, and a strange axe. The axe had a short, thick haft and a double head. Tucking the axe into his belt, he put an arrow to the string.

Fatha rode down to hail him. "A good morning to you."

The little man looked up at him for a moment, then nodded briefly. He spoke the language of the Wanderpeople, though with a strange twist.

"And a good morning it is. What might you wish here?"

Fatha smiled. "We go to the Great Wood, for lumber."

"Ah."

Fatha paused for a moment, then asked, "May we lend you a hand?"

The little man shrugged. "It is that the repairs are finished. It is that it is only a matter of refitting the wheel and lowering the wagon."

"Even so, we might lend a hand."

The little man continued to look at Fatha, apparently thinking carefully. Finally, he spoke.

"Ah. Yes, it is that I'd be glad of a hand."

So Fatha got down from his horse and walked over to the wagon. As the little man had said, there was not much left to do, but Fatha lent a pair of powerful arms to the lifting and heaving, and a few moments later the job was done. The little man extended a hand. "Thank you."

Fatha clasped the hand. "There was little to be done."

"Ah, but some would not have done even that. And now, it is that I would ask one more favour of you."

Fatha felt a chill up his back. "What favour is that?"

"That I might bring my wagon to ride at the tail of your train."

Fatha hesitated and watched a little smile appear on the lips of the little man before him. "No, you have need of no worries for me. I swear I mean no harm to your or yours."

In Fatha's mind were still the tales of the promises of the Little Brown Ones that always had a trick in them somewhere. But those promises were always faithfully carried out, weren't they? And this fellow had just sworn that he meant no harm, so---

Fatha nodded. "If you wish. Be careful, though, for some people in the train may not be so accepting as I am."

There was another little ghost of a smile. "And it is that I know that very well!"

Fatha wondered what he meant by that, but just as he never asked any of his band why they had been cast out, so he could not ask this man to say more. Something else occurred to him, though. "What is your name? I have to have something to call you."

"Ah! Duinifaire, you may call me."

"Welcome to our train, Duinifaire. I am Fatha." Something occurred to Fatha at that moment. "Tell me, Duinifaire, do you know of a water-sprite called Nik-Malo?"

"Nik-Malo? Why yes, it is that we are acquainted. Is it that you have had dealings with her?"

"From time to time, yes."

Duinifaire merely nodded. He seemed not to care particularly, and then Fatha remembered he had sworn an oath of no harm. So perhaps he did not know nor care about the jewel the nixie had given Fatha.

The outcasts continued on their way, and Duinifaire pulled in at the end.

As Fatha had predicted, not all the people in the train welcomed the little man, but as Fatha was vouching for him, none were willing to take overt action. And indeed, as time went on, most got used to having him around, and accepted him as one of them.

There were many tales concerning the Great Wood, some of them grim stories of things that lurked in the depths, waiting for unwary travellers.

It was also said that the Wanderpeople had come down out of the Great Wood many generations ago, and had taken to roaming the Great Mother Plain.

There were some among the outcasts who did not like the thought of going into the Great Wood, but they were eventually persuaded by the necessity which drove them all, and by the promise that they would remain on the edge of the wood and not go into the depths.

All the same, during the whole time that they were in the wood, most of the people were nervous and quick-tempered.

18. Gathering

While they were cutting lumber, it occurred to Fatha to make use of the opportunity. They cut more than they needed to build new wagons and brought it down to sell at one of the villages. This did not gain them a great profit, but they could trade the lumber for a pair of oxen. A spare pair of oxen was something that the band needed, for there was no telling when one of their beasts might fall sick or die, and that would leave them in a difficult situation.

The people of the village distrusted Duinifaire even more than the Plainsfolk did, though this did not stop most of them from availing themselves of his services when they found him to be skilled at such things as the mending of shoes and metal vessels.

As for Duinifaire himself, he seemed to be quite happy to follow along at the tail of the train. Although his oxen were smaller than those of the Wanderpeople, he never dropped behind, nor did his oxen appear more tired after a long day's travel.

The band continued to add to their numbers, and now they could muster a full thirty-five warriors at need, though it at least a third of those were barely old enough to be considered warriors by anyone's reckoning.

But the numbers meant they were a little safer from attacks by other Clans. The habit of caution was well-established, however. They did not raid the herds of other Clans, and were very careful during the nights when they knew other Clans were near.

In the meantime, Fatha had had another idea. He remembered the armour worn by the soldiers of Endolashan. Even though it could not stop an arrow that struck squarely, it could protect against wounds by glancing arrows, and it served to slow the arrows as well. At distances, it would probably even stop them.

Iron was not plentiful among the Wanderpeople, and to make armour shirts of that sort would be beyond their means. There were other materials, though, such as horn. Some they took from their own stocks, some they bought from the towns along the way. It was then split up and made into small plates, and they sewed these small plates onto leather shirts. Eventually, they had enough for all the warriors.

Some were not happy with it. "Fatha, this is the sort of thing that city people wear. It is heavy and unwieldy, and makes us cowards like them."

"Cowards, Jochon? How?"

"We wear these and are constantly reminded that we might be wounded. With that on our minds, how can we fight properly?"

Fatha shook his head. "Jochon, we are still few enough that we need to remember caution, at least. If the shirts give us a little protection and also remind us to þe careful, we are all of us the better for it."

"It is not manly!"

"Jochon, the warriors of Endolashan wear better armour than this all the time, and we try to avoid fighting them. Does that make them unmanly? Would you not say that the warrior who fights less because his potential foes prefer to avoid him is perhaps the better warrior?"

"Avoid fighting? Warriors avoid fighting?"

"As we have been doing the last few months, Jochon. We have been avoiding fighting because our people need us alive. But as our numbers increase, we will be less and less able to avoid fighting, even though our people need us no less. So we will wear armour to give us a better chance of coming alive out of any fight that we may get into."

Jochon retired, muttering.

There were others who did not like the notion of wearing armour, but most did not voice their objections, and the ones who did were argued down by Fatha.

It was while they were moving down well to the west of the city of Jakashan that their ability in battle was tested.

It did not come totally as a surprise; the dust-cloud in the sky told them they were near to the path of another Clan. The scouts were even more watchful than usual.

One of the scouts rode back to report that they had met a scout from the other wagon train. Each of them had ridden back to warn his own wagons, and neither had gotten close enough to see the Clan-mark of the other.

"Even then," said one of the older men, "would he not merely think that our scout was a lone outcast?"

"Possibly, but I think that our existence is probably well-known by now. Clans meet each other under truce, eat together, exchange brides, exchange news. And they also deal with the same villagers with whom we deal, so they will have heard of us. And having heard of us, I think that each time an outcast is seen riding alone, he will be suspected of being one of our scouts."

They found a small group of warriors riding toward the outcast train. Fatha sent out a small party to meet them, and that party reported back that when they came within clear sight of each other, the Clansmen shouted in alarm and rode away.

"They know we are here now. It remains to be seen what they will do about it," said Fatha.

It was only a little while later that scouts reported a somewhat larger party of Clansmen riding toward them. Fatha nodded. "Make ready," he said.

The outcasts had long ago argued out whether or not it was proper to fight from within a ring of wagons. There were still some who were not happy with the idea, but they soon realized that the danger to the outcasts was greater than to any other group, for if the outcasts met any Clan which had equal or greater numbers to theirs, they could look only to be attacked. This meant that though the outcasts might win a battle in the usual swirling cavalry melee of the Plainsfolk, given three such battles in close succession, they would be cut down by casualties to the point that they could not survive.

They herded cattle and most of the spare horses well off to the west, in the opposite direction from which the attack was expected. A few men, older men, were put to the task of keeping the animals together. They were under strict orders that if the raiders came to drive off the herds, the herdsmen should not join in battle with them, but should stand off at maximum bow range and harass them with arrows. The cattle could be recovered if the battle was won; men could be less easily replaced.

It was not very much later that the band of warriors, about forty in all, sat looking up at the circle of wagons on the hilltop. Fatha grimaced. The enemy had clearly not seen anything like this before, and they were wondering about it. And if they were given time, they might find a way to fight it.

He called three young men to him. "Get on your horses and go out there, only so close as the furthest reach of your bows, and begin raining arrows on them. I want them to be too busy to think, and irritated enough to attack without making a proper plan."

They smiled and hurried away, but he called them back. "Don't try to be heroes; once they are on their way, come back to the wagons immediately. If any of you lets himself be killed, I will never forgive you!"

They grinned, a quick flash of white teeth, and were gone. He wondered at the people he had gathered, outcasts from practically every Clan of the Wanderpeople, even some few of different tribes of the Plainsfolk, people who spoke practically nothing of the language of the Wanderpeople, and while they learned it, made do with badly pronounced words and expressive signs with the hands and face.

They were a wild lot. It was much like using wolves as a pack of hounds; he knew that violence was close beneath the surface of the mildest of them, but he had apparently mastered them for the moment. He had yet to have to use physical violence to control any of them, but that did not delude him. At any time someone might challenge him, might declare that he felt himself better fit to lead than Fatha. At present, whenever Fatha was dealing with his people, Jochon was standing behind him with a blank face and folded arms. Someday that might not be enough. In the meantime---.

The three youngsters had gone thundering down the hill now. According to instructions, they paused when they were within bow range, and launched their shafts into the group below.

He saw with approval that they were aiming mostly at the man in charge, though they never hit him. It seemed unsafe, however, for anyone to be within arm's length of him, for two men had fallen limply from their saddles before the Clansmen began to react.

Their first reaction was to launch arrows themselves, but the young men, as though Fatha were there whispering in their ears, drew back a few feet and waited. The Clansmen advanced, bringing themselves once more into bowshot, and once again the young men launched a quick arrow each and moved back.

Again the Clansmen moved up, and again the young men moved back. This time, the Clansmen moved up, unwittingly, into range of the men within the ring of wagons. Fatha shouted a command, and the outcasts began to shoot.

The Clan was now thoroughly aroused. They rode for the wagons, shouting and shooting as they came.

Though the Wanderpeople took great pride in their bowmanship, such small targets as were offered behind the wagons left them little room to demonstrate their skills. On the other hand, the men behind the wagons could shoot without the disturbance of riding a galloping horse, and their aim was deadly.

Before they had even reached the ring of wagons, the attackers were short by a third or more of their number, and began riding frantically away. "After them!" Fatha shouted. "Take prisoners!"

They had agreed on this as part of the plan, but he knew that if he didn't remind them, the outcasts might well forget in their excitement. Wagons were rolled aside, and the outcasts rode out at a gallop.

Fatha considered that this could be the time of great danger. If word of the outcast tactics got around, all a band would have to do would be to feign flight while they still retained most of their numbers, then turn on their pursuers. They would have to be wary of that. He went riding out with the rest, leaving behind a few previously assigned to guard the wagons.

19. The Mark

The prisoners stood quietly in the light of the fires, waiting for their fate. They expected death, probably a painful and humiliating death, but that did not show on their faces. There were seven of them, six young men and one older man, and some of their faces showed the signs of the struggle they had put up before being captured.

Fatha stepped out in front of them and spoke to them. "You may set your minds at rest. We do not desire your deaths, though you desired ours. Perhaps you still do. What we wish is for you to take a message for us."

"Message?" The older man spat on the ground. "Take your own messages! We are not your servants, outcast filth!"

Fatha turned to look at him and smiled, though there was no humour in the smile.

"Whoever said we would ask you to take the message? You will take the message, whether you choose to or not." He made a sign, and immediately men of the outcast band got up behind each of the prisoners, gripping them.

"I am going to take a knife," Fatha said, "And mark each of you with a cut on the cheek. After that, you will be free to go back to your Clan. But you should remember this: The next time we fight a battle, if we capture any man with a scar on his cheek, then we will deface that man's Clan-mark, making him an outcast himself. Oh, quite possibly your Clan will recognize that you are not truly outcast, but it will still mean that you will always have to have a friend with you to explain it to strangers that you meet. And who would give his daughter to a man who might be mistaken for an outcast and killed on sight? Think of that when next you ride out to battle."

Fatha had first considered defacing the Clan-marks of any captives taken, but had decided that a warning might be more useful. And if there was a warning, it should be more than mere words, which could be ignored; he would write his warning on the cheek of each man.

When he had done, he spoke again. "You may go now. We want to live and be let to live, but if we must fight, then we shall fight, and we shall do whatever is necessary. Go."

The older man was still looking at Fatha, and Fatha could tell by his expression that he, for one, would not only disregard the warning, but would specifically flout it if given a chance. Well, that must be faced when the time came. He looked around again. The prisoners' cheeks were covered with blood, almost as though they had been made outcasts already. He shuddered slightly, as though at a vision of a terrible future.

The prisoners were seen off, to be escorted to a point somewhere near to their own wagons, and let go there. Fatha turned to his own bed. Anger was burning in him, and he felt himself wishing he had not only defaced the clan-marks of the prisoners but killed them, and made a raid on their wagons while they were still upset from the results of their own raid. He wanted to kill, to destroy, to burn.

Narolen came into the wagon. "Fiyo?"

He whirled. "What?"

She flinched slightly from the look on his face, but held her ground. "Fiyo, you are upset."

He merely looked at her without answering.

"Do you even know why? I mean, the real reason why?"

"Because I have done foolishly today. I have sent off seven enemies of our band to return someday and attack us again. I ought to have killed them all. And so I am angry."

She shook her head. "Not really. What has happened is that you have been reminded of what we are. We are outcasts, and the hand of every man is against us. Worse, you have been reminded that you were made an outcast for false reasons, because someone trapped you into a situation which appeared bad, and because most of the people were willing to believe the worst about you.

"So now this all comes back to you, whether you know it or not, and makes you angry, so angry that you will shout at your best friends."

Fatha stood silent for a bit, thinking over what Narolen had said. At the end, he had to admit that she was probably right. "I'm sorry, Naro."

She smiled. "Fiyo, if I had thought it was really me you were angry at, I would have taken a horse and ridden away. I know why you were angry, so you need not apologize."

He shook his head. "I ought to even more to apologize in that case, Naro, because it is you who must suffer for my bad temper."

She smiled again. "So long as you are out of your bad temper now. Good night, Fatha."

"Good night, Narolen."

20. The First Rumour of the Krondir

They moved their wagons the next day. There was no assurance that the Clansmen would not feel insulted by Fatha's warning and launch another attack; it therefore made no sense to sit and wait within their striking range.

They stopped to do a little trading at a small village between Jakashan and Endolashan. Their herds had now grown to the point where it was possible to think about doing more than merely slaughtering those who seemed less likely to survive further travelling, so they now had a few hides to trade. They had also a few spare horses, though they had some misgivings about parting with horses.

In the village of Arik's Ford, a shallow spot in a small stream, there lived a man who dealt in most goods that people bought or sold.

He would occasionally take a trip to one of the cities, usually Jakashan, to replenish his supplies of those things which were not readily available locally.

He was swarthy, black-bearded, and stocky. He was well-fed without being fat, and his name was Udor.

After they had done their trading, they spent a little time passing whatever news had come their way.

"You have come from the north?" Udor asked.

"From the north and the west."

"Have you seen anything of the Krondir?"

"Krondir? No, who or what are they?"

Udor leaned back in his rickety wooden chair. "Well, there's a story that just this summer some people came down from northeast of the Great Wood. The Krondir seem like Plainsfolk, but they carry their families and belongings in big carts. They're short and have yellow skin, with practically no beard, so I hear. They speak a strange language, and they're said to have raided and destroyed a couple of villages north of Jakashan."

Fatha shook his head. "No, we've heard nothing of that."

"Not surprising, if you come from the northwest. They're still well north of Jakashan yet. The King of Jakashan is supposed to be sending an army against them."

Fatha shrugged. "No cause for us to worry. We are going south."

Udor nodded. "But eventually you will be going back up in that direction, as you do each year. What if the Krondir inhabit that entire part of the land?"

Fatha shrugged again. "Why then, we shall see what we shall see. If we leave them alone, perhaps they will leave us alone."

"Perhaps."

One night, after they had swung down again to follow the coast of the Bright Sea, Duinifaire approached Fatha. "It is that we will be seeing trouble, Fatha."

"Trouble?"

"Yes."

"What sort of trouble?"

"Great trouble. It is that we will be pursued by beings of great strangeness."

"Strange beings? What strange beings, Duinifaire? Must I coax it out of you one word at a time?"

A slight smile touched the small man's thick features. "I am sorry. It is that I know too little. I can only say that beasts of strangeness will be on our track, and soon."

"Oh. And can you say what we should do about it?"

Again came the slight smile. "I can say that you should be warning the people and trying to keep the wagons together. It is that I believe I can protect us, at least from the worst."

Fatha was not yet satisfied. "Why should these beasts be following us?"

Fatha caught a quick glimpse of something in the little man's face, and had a feeling that Duinifaire could have said more than he did. "Well, as to that, I may not say. They seek something, perhaps, or someone?

What should concern you, Fatha, is that they come."

Something occurred to Fatha. "Is it you that they seek, Duinifaire?"

Duinifaire smiled broadly at that, and there seemed to be a little relief in his voice. Here was something which he could answer freely and clearly. "Me? Ah, no, by the Clan-spirit, no, it is not me that they seek."

"But you do know of their coming?"

Duinifaire shrugged. "It is in their nature and in mine that I should know of their presence. And it is in my nature that I should be able to deal with such as they. Only keep the people from fear."

"When?"

"Soon. Tonight, perhaps, or tomorrow."

Fatha passed the word to his people. Some were concerned to be told only that they should not fear, and wanted to know more. Fatha, who could only pass on what he had been told by Duinifaire, was not much more content, but could only assure them that the little man had assured them of their own safety if they did not let fear get the better of them.

Few of them rested well that night, though nothing untoward happened.

In the middle of the next day, scouts reported that a single wagon was approaching them. Fatha sent off two men to see who they might be, and the word came back. It was another family of outcasts who had heard of Fatha's band and wished to join him.

This was something new; hitherto it had been a case of coming on a family or two by accident, and convincing them to join. Now, it appeared, people were seeking them out.

That evening, after the sun had fully set, they noticed a glow in the east. It was yellowish-green and seemed to be just above the horizon. Fatha sought out Duinifaire.

"Does this have anything to do with the strange beasts you have been warning us about?"

"It may, it very well may do."

"You seem very calm if these beasts are so much to be dreaded."

Duinifaire smiled. "It is that there is nothing to be gained by panic and excitement. If I can deal with them, and it is that I think it likely that I can, then there is nothing to be feared."

The glow intensified and drew nearer. With it came a faint and far-off sound of the baying of hounds, and there was something in the sound of that baying which caused even the boldest to shiver with fear. "Hold them together!" said Duinifaire to Fatha. "If they keep together, it is that I can protect them; if they scatter, they are all doomed!"

Fatha turned to his people. "Hold firm! Stay together, all of you! Duinifaire can protect us!" He put more confidence into his voice than he felt.

The glow came rapidly nearer and nearer and the sound of the hounds was louder and clearer. There was a note in it that penetrated to the very bones, and terror struck them all. There was a movement among the people, but Fatha was there, fighting back his own fear, touching, reassuring, and once or twice even taking hold of people to prevent their flight.

Then the glow came up over the nearest rise and they could see the hounds, hounds large as a wagon, hounds that glowed with a yellowish-green glow, hounds that howled with a promise of a dreadful fate, and behind whose eyes lurked something to cause the bravest heart to quail.

The hounds swept up the hill toward the wagons, and Duinifaire slowly raised his hands out from his sides, palms forward. Almost as though they saw nothing but an obstruction in their path, the pack parted to right and left to go round the wagons. A smell came with them, a stench of the grave and of other horrible things.

One young man broke and ran for his horse, flung himself on it, and rode out. Fatha grabbed two others before they could follow suit and saw Jochon subduing another. The fleeing man went only a few paces into the night before the hounds reached him. There was a shriek of pure terror from the horse and a wail from the man, a wail which faded off as into great distance. The sound of the hounds faded off into the distance as rapidly as it had come, and was gone altogether. Duinifaire lowered his arms.

The night was still and quiet.

21. The Jewel of Nik-Malo

The band was nervous for the next three days. No sign was ever seen of the young man who had fled, nor of his horse. Fatha asked Duinifaire, but could get no satisfactory answer.

"What happened to that young man?"

"Ah," said Duinifaire, and hesitated. "It is that it is difficult to say."

"Why?"

"Because of the circumstances, because of the hounds and what be the hounds."

"And what are the hounds?"

"Ah." Again the hesitation. "It is that it is difficult to explain."

"Why is it so difficult to explain? Duinifaire, again I am having to pull information out of you one word at a time."

The little man spread his hands expressively. "Fatha, if it should be that you were talking to a man who was blind, how would you explain the colour blue?"

Fatha thought about that for a moment, then smiled. "I think I see what you mean. What can you explain?"

"Well, it is that the hounds are beings, beings from a world beyond this one. It is that they can be called into this one if someone knows how to do so. When it is that they are set to hunt, they are usually set at a distance from their quarry so that the fear of the hounds can do its work before arrive the hounds themselves."

"So, someone is seeking to destroy us?"

"Not exactly. It is that they are seeking something of you, but your destruction would be only incidental."

"Then what do they seek?"

The little man looked Fatha full in the face. "It is that they seek the jewel that Nik-Malo gave to you."

"The jewel? But why?"

Duinifaire stood quiet. "It has to do with wars and battles, with fights and struggles in realms you know not at all. It was given to you as a trust, but by whatever means, its presence was revealed to her enemies. And it is that I have come to help you protect it."

Fatha stood silent for a time, considering. "And the hounds are among the least of the beings that will be sent to fetch the nixie's jewel? Best then that I cast it away and let them find it, rather than endanger all my people."

The small man merely looked at Fatha.

"No, of course I cannot do that; I made a promise, a matter of honour. I suppose that the alternative is to leave myself, with the jewel, and protect the people."

"So, then? It is that you trust me so little? Fatha, the people need you. Without you, they would fall apart and become prey for any who seek their harm. Did I not tell you that I will protect you? Is it that you did not believe me?"

Fatha sighed. "So be it. But I will not tell this to all the people."

Duinifaire grinned. "As well you do not. Most do not have hearts like yours."

Fatha told no one of his talk with Duinifaire, not wishing to add to the burdens of the people. However, the people still had their worries. One man eventually came to Fatha and said, "I worry about that Small One in our midst."

"You worry about him? Why?"

"What might he do to us? It is well known that he and his kind are not lovers of human beings."

"If he meant us harm, surely all he need do was let the hounds have us."

"But perhaps he has a worse fate in mind for us."

"Nonsense! When has he ever shown any harmful intention toward us?"

"But do you really trust one who has the power to turn aside the hounds as he did the other night? If he can cause them to turn aside, what else might he do?"

Fatha shook his head. "Nonsense!" he repeated. "If he is ever shown to do anyone harm, come and tell me. Until then, let it be."

"You may be willing to let it be, but some others may not!"

Fatha looked the other man directly in the eye. "If you wish to leave the train, you may do so, but I will not have you or anyone spreading tales of discouragement and division among us. Do you understand that?"

The man shuffled his feet a little and looked down. "All right, but it is on your head."

"Of course." Fatha smiled. "Did I ever say that it would be otherwise? I am the leader, and my responsibility is to lead, and I am to be held accountable for my leading, for good or for ill."

Twice more in the next few days, people joined them. Once it was a young man with only a horse and the equipment he carried, the second time it was a man with a family, and three cows. The young man was very young, very brash, and the cuts on his face were not yet healed. He asked to see the chief of the band and was brought to Fatha. He surveyed Fatha a little doubtfully.

"By the teeth and toes of the Clan-spirit, you are not at all what I had expected."

"And what had you expected?"

"For a leader of a band of outcasts? Probably someone who was taller, wider, and older, quite able to knock heads together to make people behave. Instead, I find someone who looks more like a father, and a young father at that."

Fatha shrugged. "I suppose I do as well as anyone. Do you wish to join us?"

"Oh, yes. You are keeping this band together despite your looks, so it must be safe enough."

"You have no idea how happy I am to have gained your approval." Fatha said. His sarcasm seemed to have no effect on the young man.

Jochon, who had been standing behind Fatha in his usual place, waited until the young man had left to express his opinion. "That fellow needs to be taken down a peg or two."

"Quite likely. He is young, and there is plenty of time for it. He will learn, after a while."

On the night after the older man with the wagon had joined them, when Fatha was preparing for bed, Narolen spoke to him. "Fiyo?"

"Yes?"

"Come into my bed."

It caught him by surprise, though he had been thinking about it from time to time. "Now?"

"Now."

Afterwards, he asked her, "Why tonight?"

She smiled at him, a smile barely seen in the dimness inside the wagon. "Because today has shown that we are attracting new people, that our band is growing because people have heard of us. And this means that it is a little more safe for us to think of a family ourselves, now that we can protect ourselves from most enemies.

"You have done well, Fatha."

He could think of no answer to that.

22. The Krondir

The outcasts continued to hear word of the Krondir, from caravans who crossed their path, from villages at which they traded. Apparently, the King of Jakashan had fought a battle with the Krondir. Beyond that, there was no sure news, for some insisted he had won and others that he had lost, and some even said that he had barely escaped the field of battle with his life.

By the time they came near Dannon-ska, the information was a little more certain. There had been a battle, the army of Jakashan had been defeated, practically wiped out, and the Krondir were driving their carts under the very walls of the city. They had even been reported a little to the east of Hadar-esh.

The King of Dannon-ska was even sending out agents to approach certain Clans of the Wanderpeople to ask them to serve in his army. This sort of thing would happen from time to time; certain of the Kings would become involved in wars and, seeking to increase their army, would send messengers out to the plains.

The outcasts were not approached, being a small and little-known group. Fatha considered for a time offering his services, but he realized they would not likely be welcome. The people of the city would know quite well the strife that would come of putting a band of outcasts in the same army as Clansmen.

They had three more battles with Clans of the Wanderpeople. The first two they won from their wagon-circle, the third was a hard-fought skirmish during a week when the ground was too damp to put up clouds of dust, which meant that a fairly large wagon-train came too near to be avoided, and the warriors appeared too suddenly for the outcasts to be able to go into their circle.

The armour of the outcasts served them well that day, for they lost only five men, while the enemy lost significantly higher.

In each of the three battles, prisoners were taken and were warned and marked on the cheek.

Near Dannon-ska, three wagons joined them. Three middle-aged men, who had been cast out some years ago, had gone to the city. There they had learned trades and prospered, even marrying and having children. But they had all longed for the life of the Plains, and when the story came to them of the band of outcasts wandering the plains, they had saved up what money they could, bought wagons and teams, and set out to find Fatha and his band.

They were well to the east of Hadar-esh when they first came upon the Krondir. The scouts out in front reported a party of five men on horseback riding in their direction, so Fatha had his warriors prepare for battle, just in case.

He himself rode out with Jochon and a few others to see who and what these people might be. They first caught sight of the strangers from a long distance, across a valley. They rode carefully forward, weapons ready. The others had apparently seen them as well, and came to meet them.

These were no sort of Plainsfolk that the outcasts had ever seen before. They were shorter than the Wanderpeople, more broadly built, with neither beards nor moustaches, and their eyes were strangely narrow. For weapons, they had bows of the same sort as the Wanderpeople, and short, curved swords.

The two groups looked at each other for a while, then finally the man who was apparently the leader of the strangers said, with a very heavy accent, "Who are you?"

23. Soldiers of Endolashan

"We are of the Wanderpeople," Fatha answered. "Who are you?"

The other ignored the question. "What is Wanderpeople?"

"Our tribe, our people, call themselves so. Who are you?"

"We are Krondir. You hear of us?"

"A little. Why have you come?"

"We come because we go where we want! We need no permission from some fat fellow who lives behind walls and need no permission from any scum of this country. We go where we wish, and it's best you stay out of our way!"

Fatha could sense Jochon's anger rising to rage, so he calmly said, "Perhaps, being that there are but five of you, you ought not to talk so boldly."

"Hah! Few of you as well, and even if we die, more of us come looking."

Fatha shrugged. "There is plenty of room on the Great Mother Plain, fellow. What is your name?"

"I am Tiondak, and you?"

"My name is Fatha. So, Tiondak, as I have said, there is plenty of room on the Great Mother Plain. We go our way, you may go yours, and there need be no trouble between us."

"Trouble? Krondir fear no trouble. You stay out of our path, we maybe leave you alone. You stray into our path, we run over you like a bug."

"Then beware, lest the bug be a scorpion and bite your foot, Tiondak."

The Krondir's hand tightened on his bow. "You threaten?"

"No more than you. Let us remain at peace, Tiondak; war would be a hazard for all." He recognized by now that talking with the other man would only lead to wrangling and bickering, perhaps eventually fighting. He turned his horse and rode away.

As they went, Jochon came up beside him. "By the toes and teeth of the Clan-spirit, Fatha, that is a very haughty little man! And you let him speak so!"

"What good would it do to begin a fight, Jochon? Words will not hurt us, and as I have said, there is plenty of room. Let them be, and if they begin seeking trouble, then we will give them all the trouble they need."

The outcasts swung their wagons far to the south, hoping to avoid further contact with the Krondir. The second day after their meeting with Tiondak and his men, they came upon the remains of a wagon train. It had numbered about forty wagons and had apparently been surprised by an overwhelming force of enemies. The men had fought, of course, but it appeared that surprise and numbers had defeated them.

The wagons had been looted and burned, the women and children mostly slain, though the number of dead seemed a little small for the number of wagons, which meant that some must have been taken off into captivity. Many of the oxen and cattle had been wantonly slaughtered as well, with a few strips of meat cut off and apparently roasted over the fires of the burning wagons. The rest had been driven off.

Silently, they swung a little further in out of the regular path.

Six days later, the scouts rode back to report a small band of Krondir coming up, about forty strong. There was not time to circle the wagons and make proper preparations, so Fatha gathered his warriors and rode out to meet the foreigners.

The leader of this band was a little taller and a little more slender than most. He and three others met Fatha, Jochon, and Temo halfway between the two bodies.

"Who are you?" he demanded.

"I am Fatha, leader of this band. And you?"

"I Tialka of the Krondir. This land our land. What do here?"

"We pass through, as always."

Tialka laughed. "You do not pass through as always. This time you pay to pass."

"Pay?"

"Yes. Our land, you pass through, you pay. You refuse?"

Fatha considered that. Jochon spoke at his right elbow. "Fatha, you will not pay! We can beat this band of rabble easily!"

"Perhaps we can, Jochon, but what happens when the remnants of this band go back for reinforcements? Remember how slowly ox-drawn wagons move? We won't escape. Best to pay and survive."

"No!"

"Jochon, we will pay. And we will look to the future to see what must be done."

Jochon subsided, muttering. Tialka obviously could not follow their conversation properly, for he waited for Fatha to speak. "What is the payment?"

Tialka grinned maliciously. "Forty cattle."

At that point, Fatha almost refused. Forty cattle was a substantial portion of their herd, and not something they could afford to give up easily. He recalled his discussion with his father that day outside the walls of Dannonska and felt the leadership of the band heavy on his shoulders. Finally, he nodded. "Forty cattle."

Tialka said something to one of his men in their own language, and that man went racing back to the main force. A moment later, ten of them rode rapidly down to the herd, picking out cattle and driving them away.

Tialka grinned again. "Maybe we see you again, Fatha. Maybe we like you cattle." He wheeled his horse and rode away.

Grimly, the outcasts went on their way. They were somewhat to the south of Jakashan when they met with a merchant caravan. The merchant, a big black-bearded man by the name of Yistar, seemed happy to see them.

"You are west of the road, are you not?" asked Fatha.

The merchant's face went grim. "I am. Those accursed Krondir watch the roads, and sometimes they let a caravan through for a price, sometimes they take what they want and kill all the people."

"Ah!"

"Indeed. And now that Jakashan is fallen, there is nothing to hold them back."

"Jakashan fallen?"

"Oh indeed! Last week, it happened, and I was one of a few who came out before the Krondir could come in. I understand that the King of Jakashan has fled to Endolashan, to make obeisance to the King of Kings and hope for an army to help take his city back."

"Worse than I had thought, then! Is there no end to these arrogant Krondir?"

Yistar laughed. "Arrogant indeed. For all their talk of 'We go where we wish,' you know why they come here? Back where they live, they had five good years, years in which their tribes and cattle prospered. Then they had five bad years, so bad that the land could not support their increased numbers. In the fighting for scarce grazing and water, these are the ones who lost out, who were driven from their lands to find new homes."

"How do you know all this?"

"Ah, merchants come and merchants go, even into far-away lands. And where they go, they keep their eyes and ears open."

Fatha nodded.

"Do you travel so far as Endolashan?" asked Yistar.

"Probably not. Our people are not well-liked at Endolashan."

"They may like you better these days. They will be needing fighting men to face the Krondir, and they will be taking whoever they can get. There is money to be made thus, Fatha."

Fatha considered this for a short time, then shook his head. "No, though I would like to do something to take the smirk off some arrogant Krondir faces, perhaps it would not be worth working for the King of Kings."

"So. In any case, would you mind if I ride with you for a few more miles? If there are Krondir in the neighbourhood, they may be less willing to attack so large a force."

"So long as the dust does not bother you, you are welcome."

A few days later, but still well before they would swing west away from Endolashan, they were met by a force of fifty heavy cavalry of Endolashan. The leader was a big man, as arrogant as any Krondir, though he spoke the language of the Wanderpeople tolerably well.

"Who are you?"

“I am Fatha.”

“You have seen the Krondir to the north?”

“Yes.”

“Ha! How far?”

“A week, ten days.”

“Good. The King of Kings is gathering armies, and he wishes you to join.”

“He does? How does the King of Kings know me?”

The officer grinned mockingly. “He does not, but I have been bidden to say thus to every group of nomads I meet.”

“Ah. Well, I fear that I will not be able to join your armies.”

The officer raised his brows. “No? I fear that I cannot accept that answer. Shall we say, then, that either you will join us or you will suffer? And if you do join us, you will be well paid.”

Fatha looked at the force of heavy cavalry, considered what their chances were against such a force, even if behind the circle of wagons.

“Of course, the King of Kings needs food for his army. Say that we either take you for the army, or your cattle for food?”

The armoured men could drive the cattle off, and the only way that the outcasts could get them back would be to come out after them, which would lead to a battle in the open. In such a battle, the heavy cavalry had the advantage. This officer clearly knew something of how to deal with the clans of the Wanderpeople.

“Well?” demanded the officer, raising his hand to signal his troops.

24. Battle

The armies of Endolashan marched northward. There were upwards of twenty thousand warriors, with at least that many camp followers. The warriors were of numerous sorts. Regular soldiers of Endolashan made up the largest contingent, then a large body of warriors of the Wanderpeople, recruited much in the way the outcasts had been recruited. This meant that there were some fifty or more small Clans, each supported by its own wagons and families. There were other contingents, short stocky men from down on the east coast of the Bright Sea, armed with bow and sword, tall swordsmen from the lands to the east of the city of Endolashan, men of the west mounted on little horses, and others.

The outcasts had had to be kept separate from the other Wanderpeople, as Fatha had predicted, and there was even some discussion of the desirability of dismissing them altogether. It had been decided, however, that no contingent, however small, could be dispensed with in the upcoming fight. They kept the outcasts near the front of the column, their warriors used extensively in scouting.

There was also a small contingent of heavy cavalry kept near to the outcasts' wagons; Fatha might have felt offended at this if it had not been that there were similar contingents near each of the other groups of Wanderpeople. An officer of Endolashan accompanied each group of Wanderpeople to pass orders and messages.

They had even been favoured with a visit from the King of Kings himself. One day, a large four-wheeled chariot came by the wagons of the outcasts. Thirty troopers escorted it, all in armour decorated with gold, silver, and jewels. The chariot itself had a cover over it, a cover resembling a large squarish tent made of cloth dyed purple and crimson and gold. There was no way to see who was inside, but the officer with the outcasts, a man named Vrast, drew in a hissing breath and muttered, "The Great One!"

The chariot paused in its progress, for there was not room on the road to get past the wagons of the outcasts. The leader of the escort troop, a large man with a carefully curled black beard, began shouting at them. Unlike most Endolashans of his rank, he spoke the language of the Wanderpeople quite well.

"You up there! Get this filth-ridden wagon out of the way! Off the road, I say! You, there, driver of this rotting hulk! Are you deaf and blind too? Move!"

As the wagon creaked its way off to the side of the road, the curtains of the great tent on the chariot opened and a pudgy face appeared. It was surmounted by a crown made of long, thin plaques of ivory, joined with gold wire and rounded at the tops. A hand weighted with huge rings of gold and silver, each with a jewel of some sort, held the curtains aside.

"Mardrast!" he said, in a somewhat querulous voice, then went on with a question of some sort.

The officer in charge of the escort turned and, looking down at the ground in front of him, answered the question soothingly.

The querulous voice spoke again, and a jewelled finger pointed at Fatha.

Vrast, looking down himself, was pulling at Fatha's sleeve and frantically whispering, "Look down, fool! Look down or we're doomed!"

He did not understand the reasons behind Vrast's agitation, but he understood well enough the urgency in his tone. He heard Mardrast speaking again, at length still and soothingly, then the man in the chariot withdrew behind the curtains again. The vehicle moved on.

Mardrast, leader of the escort, drew aside and spoke quickly to Vrast, using the language of the Wanderpeople. "Best you should teach these plains-roving scum how to handle themselves in the presence of the Great One. I may not always be around to intercede."

"Yes, Lord."

Mardrast grunted and rode away.

Vrast turned to Fatha and spoke. "You heard all that?"

"Yes. He spoke in my language so that I should know not only that I had done wrong, but also how little he thinks of me. But I think it would be a long time before they begin killing off the chiefs of their warriors; they need soldiers too badly."

Vrast nodded. "They need you badly, but the Great One's moods are chancy. If you upset him, or if he is upset by something about you, and if he decides that he wishes to have you executed, then Mardrast may not be able to talk him out of it."

"What did the Great One say?"

"First of all, he asked what was happening, why they had stopped. Mardrast told him it was a mere matter of barbarians blocking the road. He then asked why 'that fellow' by which he meant you, was staring at him.

"One thing you should know in particular, Fatha, if you should ever find yourself in the presence of the King of Kings again, look down at the ground and continue to look down until he invites you to look up. Even then, do not look him in the face for any length of time; it is considered rude to the point of being insulting."

"And if the King of Kings feels I am insulting him, he could order me put to death?"

"Exactly. And while Mardrast would prefer to keep chiefs of contingents from being executed, he is not willing to jeopardize his own standing in order to do so. So if he sees that the Great One is intent on punishing someone, he will quickly come round to seeing just how criminal was that person's behaviour."

Fatha nodded. "I will try to be careful, then. And I will warn all my people."

There was a little knoll along the bank of the River Korba, just south of the city of Jakashan, and there they met the Krondir. For three days they had been meeting with Krondir scouts and patrols, skirmishing with them, taking and causing a few casualties. But they could not gain any idea about the whereabouts or the strength of the main Krondir force.

Mardrast and some of the other Endolashan commanders were not pleased with this. Some even muttered about betrayal by the scouts and Fatha forbore to point out that he and his people had not been asked if they wished to take part in this war. Such a comment would only make the situation worse.

The Krondir army waiting for them by the knoll was approximately equal to them in size, but the Krondir were all horsemen while the army of Endolashan was composed of contingents of cavalry and infantry.

The commanders of Endolashan were quite confident. They considered the Krondir to be barbarians, and therefore of little account as warriors. Pointing out that these same Krondir had twice defeated armies of Jakashan did not seem to make much of an impression; their response was usually to say scornfully, "Oh, yes, Jakashan armies."

The Krondir lined up facing southward, far enough away from the riverbank to avoid the soft ground there. The army of Endolashan lined up facing them, with the heavy cavalry contingents on the right wing, lighter cavalry next, all the way down to the infantry on the left wing armed with shield, spear and sword.

Fatha's contingent, rather than being grouped with the rest of the Wanderpeople, had been placed on the left flank, behind the infantry, to support them with arrows. Fatha found himself angered by this, though when he considered it, he had to admit that placing the outcasts with the other Wanderpeople would be a source of potential danger.

An officer wearing the uniform of the bodyguard of the King of Kings came round to speak to Vrast. When he had gone, Vrast turned to Fatha. "We will advance at a walk to within charging distance. The rest of us will hold the Krondir on our front while the heavy cavalry will crush their left wing, then swing round and roll them up from the flank."

"An interesting plan," said Fatha. "But what if the Krondir refuse to be held, crushed, or rolled up?"

"What do you mean?"

"They are on horseback. If they decide to move away, not to close with us, what then?"

Vrast shrugged. "Mardrast and the people who think up battle plans have more experience of battle than I, or perhaps even you, Fatha. And if this plan does not succeed, I expect they will have some other plan in mind."

"I hope so."

There was no time for more talk, for the signal-horn blew and the army moved.

They went forward at a steady pace, keeping their alignment, underofficers maintaining a constant rhythm of "Left, right, left, right!" The horses of the Wanderpeople sensed the tension in the air and wanted to run. They had to be reined in sharply, and it was because of this that Fatha missed the beginning of the Krondir maneuver.

He knew first that there was shouting from the ranks of the Endolashan army, and when he looked up, the Krondir had divided in two parts and were riding away to left and right, each segment curling southward as it rode. Their intention was clearly to flank the army of Endolashan.

It was a tactic which would have been dangerous against a more maneuverable force, or even against a force where the commander could move a significant part of his troops individually. In such a case, one flank could have held defensively against one part of the Krondir while the other flank defeated the Krondir facing them, then turned to attack what remained.

As it was, however, most of the army turned to face the flanking forces, and there was much confusion in the centre where no one could decide where the force should divide. On the right flank, the heavy cavalry went charging off after the Krondir, only to become bogged down in the marshy ground next to the river's edge.

The Krondir had some difficulty there as well, and the heavy cavalry even caught the rearmost elements of them struggling through the ground, which had been turned into a quagmire by the hooves of the horses ahead of them.

A few heavy cavalrymen fell to arrows, but their heavy horses crashed into the almost stationary enemy, long lances doing severe damage. The Krondir, not equipped to match them hand to hand, suffered badly.

But only for a short time. The Krondir who had already ridden past turned even further, then swept suddenly down on the flank and rear of the heavy cavalry. They rode in close, releasing clouds of arrows, then after a moment spent skirmishing, rode away.

By this time, Fatha and the people on his wing had little leisure to view what was happening elsewhere. Fatha, recognizing the maneuver even as it was happening, got his men turned around. Vrast, a little unsure what to do without orders from the army commanders, dithered, but could not prevent them.

"Here they come!" shouted Fatha, realizing as he did so that he needn't have bothered speaking; anyone with eyes could see the obvious. The Krondir would not likely try to come to grips for more than a moment; their advantages were their mobility and their bows, and they were not foolish enough to give those up.

In a normal situation, Fatha and his men would have fought much as the Krondir; riding in, shooting arrows, skirmishing momentarily, then riding away again in feigned flight. The victory usually went to the side which best feigned flight, drawing the enemy to scatter in pursuit. At that time, the fleeing force would suddenly turn and destroy the pursuers in small groups before they could reform.

But in this situation, Fatha and his outcasts had little room to maneuver, with the river and the confused Endolashan army behind them and the outnumbering force of the Krondir before them.

Fatha ordered his men forward. He could see the hairless Krondir faces in the moving wall of men and horses before him. He could hear their shrill cries in their own incomprehensible tongue. Like the outcasts, they were now guiding their mounts with their knees, bending their bows and preparing to loose their arrows.

"Loose!" Fatha shouted. It was a little far at present, but they were certain to take casualties in the first vollies of the Krondir and it would be best to do some damage of their own before that time.

The arrow-storm came whistling down among the outcasts now, and Fatha hunched his shoulders as if against a heavy rain, knowing that it would help not at all. Somehow he remained unhit, though he saw others fall.

Now they were coming too close for bows, and it would be sword work all the way. Cut, slash, thrust, parry, dodge, and cut again. He shouted as loud as any in the hammering din, and some part of his mind recognized that Jochon was right behind him, grimly striking to right or left.

He noticed that some of the Krondir were using a looped rope which they would cast over the head of an opponent, then jerk him from the saddle, or even merely to entangle his sword-arm to give them the opportunity for a first strike.

At close range, the horn armour of the outcasts proved its worth repeatedly, for though it was not impregnable, it would still turn many otherwise fatal blows.

A shrieking whistle sounded again and again above the din; suddenly the Krondir were turning and fleeing. A few of Fatha's men, the younger ones, went rushing after them, but some older and more experienced warriors brought them back.

Fatha looked around. The field was a mass of dead and wounded men. An infantry behind which they had marched up the field were practically wiped out. The rest were now taking the opportunity of this respite to take flight. Fatha knew they would not get far; such unorganized rabble would be ridden over in one charge of the Krondir.

A little further down were the remains of a contingent of archers; they had given a good account of themselves, from the look of the field around them. When the Krondir came back, even they would not survive for more than a few moments. He swung round, looking for Vrast, and found him near his own left elbow.

"We have to retreat," Fatha said. "They have us disorganized now, and the next charge they will destroy us."

"We cannot retreat. The King of Kings--
-"

"Is already fleeing. Look!" Fatha gestured. It was true. The chariot, with a dozen or so golden-armoured horsemen around it, was racing back down the road, bouncing and jouncing toward whatever safety there might be to the south.

"It is up to us to save ourselves. We have only a little time before the Krondir come back. Let us go!"

Vrast hesitated, then nodded. "If it must be so. But how can we survive, even if we retreat?"

"If we gather whatever remnants of the army, we can find. Those archers over there, for instance. Come on, all of you!" he called to his men.

Seeing the band of horsemen bearing down on them, the archers readied their weapons again. They were only dissuaded from loosing arrows by Vrast, riding forward alone and convincing him that these were friends.

Their commander was a little taller than the rest of them, but was still short and stocky, fair-skinned and red-haired, his face and arms a mass of freckles. There was something in his eyes that made Fatha realize that here was a man who would not let himself be defeated easily.

He could not speak the language of the Wanderpeople, so Vrast had to translate between him and Fatha. "Tell him we want to get off this field alive, and we would welcome his assistance."

"He says that he doubts if any of us can get off this field alive, and he is not willing to let himself take an arrow in the back running away."

"We will not run, I assure you. We want to take our wagons and families with us, and the oxen do not run very fast. If there are enough of us, we can stand them off for a time and continue to move southward. They will have enough easy meat, like those fellows," he thrust his chin toward the infantry who were fleeing, being dogged by a large party of Krondir. "By the time they decide to come for us, we can be far enough to the south that they themselves will be more scattered."

The commander of the archers looked uncertain. Fatha said, "Make up your mind now; the Krondir will be coming back soon, and we have no time to argue."

Vrast passed that ultimatum to him, and the commander spent a moment thinking, then nodded sharply.

"Good," said Fatha. "Let us march."

There was still a battle going on at the riverbank where the remnants of the Endolashan heavy cavalry were being wiped out by the Krondir. The Krondir were coming back again on the other flank, having discovered that their feigned flight had drawn no one off.

"Be ready," shouted Fatha. "When they come within range, loose arrows!" Vrast passed that message on to the commander of the archers, who nodded grimly.

The enemy came sweeping up, closer, closer. Fatha shouted a command, and the whole group stopped, turned, and loosed arrows. The nomads were caught by surprise; men and horses went down, but they were by no means defeated. They loosed arrows of their own, and once more the outcasts were standing in a whistling shower of missiles.

But the outcasts and the foot-archers were still shooting, and more and more Krondir saddles were emptied. This was not the sort of fight the Krondir favoured, and before even coming to grips, they sheered off and rode down into some of the other Endolashan troops who were fleeing from the battle.

The outcasts and their new allies continued their march.

They had left their wagons somewhat behind the line of battle, and the Krondir had as yet been too busy with the army of Endolashan to do any plundering. Fatha was happy to see that the women and youngsters had already begun harnessing the oxen in preparation to move.

The wagons, of course, could not move very fast, but they moved. Another band of Krondir came galloping by, shooting arrows as they went. They took a few arrows in return and went off to find easier prey.

A little down the road, they passed the chariot of the King of Kings. The driver was dead, and the body of the King of Kings himself slumped halfway out of the curtains. There were three dead bodyguards in the vicinity, along with four dead Krondir.

About two dozen heavy cavalry came galloping up from behind, fleeing the battlefield. They would have ridden around the Wanderpeople, but Fatha brought his men out in front of them.

They had no leader, but a few of them spoke a little of the language of the Wanderpeople. "Get out of our way, fools! They are coming!"

"Yes, they are. We need your help; come along with us."

"Go with you? And die with you? Get out of our way!"

"You have two choices," Fatha said grimly. "You can join with us, or you can ride on and we will shoot you down as you go. Which would you prefer?"

They milled around uncertainly for a moment, then one of them spurred his horse directly at them, attempting to ride through. From Fatha's right elbow, Jochon's bow hummed, and the man went down.

"Make your choice," Fatha said.

The cavalrymen agreed to join, and the newly augmented force continued moving. The wagons had not stopped during this negotiation, so they rode to catch up. Two of the heavy cavalry did not pause upon reaching the wagons, but continued on their way, urging their horses to gallop. They were both brought down with arrows in the back before they had gone far.

Vrast looked at Fatha. "You are killing our own men!"

"I am trying to save our lives, and in the process, perhaps save theirs," Fatha answered. "If the price of it is to make examples of a few cowards, then so be it. Now let us make ready, for here comes the enemy again."

25. Retreat

The long retreat to Endolashan was not accomplished easily. There were always bands of the Krondir hovering just beyond bowshot, who would sweep down, shoot a few arrows, and be gone. Occasionally, very occasionally, a larger band would try a major attack to see if the group could be forced to disintegrate and flee, to be picked off a few at a time.

Fatha kept them together, how he was not quite sure, though he thought perhaps he had succeeded in making them more afraid of him than of the ever-present enemy.

In their flight, they gathered other small bits and pieces of the army, little groups who had survived the rout, and were glad to throw in their lot with a larger force, and sometimes parties who had to be persuaded to join.

They even gathered a few groups of the Wanderpeople with wagons, who let their fear of the Krondir overcome their distaste for the company of outcasts.

But it was a running battle all the way, and it was not too long before Fatha had to send out parties of his horsemen to loot the bodies of dead Krondir for arrows, which were running low among his forces.

But small parties of the enemy learned quickly not to approach this band of fugitives who met them and fought desperately, never giving way to panic-stricken flight, maintaining their steady pace and greeting any who came too near with showers of arrows.

But there was hardly time for two deep breaths in succession before someone shouted that the Krondir were on the horizon, and Fatha would have to go out again, encouraging and cajoling his men, sometimes even threatening them, arranging his meagre forces to meet the enemy, loosing arrows, occasionally taking part in a short, milling cavalry skirmish, then picking up arrows and preparing to do the same thing again.

Duinifaire, he noticed, was still with them. Too small to ride a horse, the little man had stayed with the wagons; but when the Krondir attacked, he plied his bow with the best of them.

On they went, mile after weary mile, always hoping that when they got over the next rise, the enemy would cease following, but always finding that the enemy was already over the next rise, waiting.

They rested at night, never for more than a few hours, moving on further southward, though oxen, men, and horses were rapidly wearying.

Then came an evening when Fatha realized they had had only three desultory attacks that day, and those by rather small bands. He hoped that this might signal the beginning of the end, but he said nothing to his people; best not get their hopes up only to have them dashed the next morning by a vast host of enemy.

And indeed, the next day, a large force of Krondir appeared on the horizon ahead of them.

The fugitives made ready to fight again; Fatha had found that the heavy cavalry, if they could come to close quarters with the Krondir, gave a good account of themselves. He had taken to putting the heavy cavalry behind his own Wanderpeople, drawing the Krondir into combat, then letting the heavy cavalry come through the ranks of the horse-archers.

The enemy came up on the run. Fatha had been in the habit of trying always to get the first volley of arrows in so they could cut down, even by a few, the number of arrows in the return volley. A few of the enemy went down, then the return volley was falling among them like a deadly sleet.

Once more, they shot into the howling horde, then the Krondir swerved off to ride down their left flank. The fugitives became to be quite adept at maneuvering as well, at always having the most men at the point of most danger. They could shoot one more volley into the enemy as they went by, and a few individual shots before the Krondir were out of range. Fatha, as usual, told off a couple of men to keep watch and warn them when the Krondir came back.

He also told of men to go out and pick up what arrows they could from the enemy dead. Like the Wanderpeople, the Krondir kept quivers strapped on their saddles under the right knee. Fatha had occasionally ordered certain men to shoot enemy horses in order to replenish their arrow-supply even minimally.

The oxen plodded on. Suddenly, a scout was back with a report. "Fatha, they stopped just over the rise and appeared to hold a meeting of some sort. After a little while, they set out again in the direction they had been going. I don't think they will be coming back."

"Good. But we can't count on that; keep a good watch anyway. We can't afford to have them surprise us."

But the Krondir did not come back. The fugitives never lost their wariness, but a few days later they came into sight of the walls of Endolashan with no further attacks.

A small party of Endolashan heavy cavalry came out to meet them, and Fatha and Vrast found it necessary to explain how they had escaped the destruction of the battlefield. The officer, one of a type which seemed to abound in the Endolashan army, with curled and oiled hair and beard and a superior disposition, commanded, "Wait here, and word from the King of Kings will be sent to you."

"The King of Kings?" asked Vrast. "If I may be so bold, who is the King of Kings?"

The officer turned a sneer on Vrast. "And who might you be?"

Vrast drew himself up. "I am Vrast kinda Vrast i Hodurnan, and I have fought my way back from a disastrous battle, bringing to the King of Kings some experienced troops. I know not how I may stand with the new King of Kings, but I am sure that between his gratitude and the honour of my family, we can teach manners to any upstart pup who has never seen a bloody blade. Now answer my question!"

The commander wilted. "The new King of Kings is Mardrast, who came back from the battle to tell how the King of Kings had died in valiant battle with the Krondir, and would have defeated them but for their numbers."

Vrast merely nodded. "Go back, then, and tell them who we are."

After the officer and his troop had left, Fatha turned to Vrast. "So we would have won, but for sheer numbers, then? As I recall it, we were outmaneuvered and smashed, and the King of Kings died when the Krondir caught up to his fleeing chariot and shot arrows into him through the fancy curtains."

"And if you wish to stay alive, Fatha, you will not mention any of that, and will warn your people as well. The King of Kings, Mardrast, will not take it kindly if anyone disputes his tale."

"Of course."

26. The Old Woman

The King of Kings requested the Wanderpeople to camp outside the city and wait for his pleasure. Certain of them would have set out for the Great Mother Plain almost at once, except that certain heavy cavalry were camped out near them. Rather than fight a costly battle with the soldiers of Endolashan, they stayed.

The King of Kings sent out officers to take from them, accounts of how they had come away from the field of battle, and after a few more days, sent out new orders.

The King of Kings had declared that because Fatha of the Outcasts ("he makes us sound like a real clan," Jochon had muttered) and his people had shown themselves to be skilled in battle against the Krondir, the same Fatha would be placed over a large band of the

Plainsfolk who would be gathered together in preparation for a fresh battle against the Krondir.

And to show that he understood the difficulties involved in setting an outcast to command several clans, he declared that any of the Plainsfolk who objected to this arrangement would be taken, bound with his family, and placed in his wagon and the wagon set on fire.

The number of Wanderpeople who had come back safe from the battle was small, but apparently the King of Kings had his troops out riding the plains, searching for others.

Fatha wondered what might happen if they should bring in the clan that had been his father's, to make them serve under the man they had cast out. Of course, that clan was a little large to be bullied into service by the Endolashan heavy cavalry, but it was possible that they might be attracted by the prospect of the wages they would receive.

They did not present Fatha with that particular problem. Though several smaller clans were gathered. There was some initial difficulty with each of them when they discovered they were to be commanded by an outcast. None of them, though, were willing to test the matter far enough to see if the King of Kings would make good his threats.

It was quite clear that the King of Kings would not be ready to fight the Krondir again for some time. Messengers were going out to all parts of the Empire to request more troops to come in; more soldiers were indeed coming in, but they came slowly. Staying in one place in this manner did not suit the Wanderpeople at all, but being subject to the whim of the King of Kings, they were forced to endure.

One morning, just as Fatha was about to set out on his usual rounds of his own people, followed by a visit to the other clans presently under his orders, Narolen called to him.

"Fiyo, could I speak with you a moment?"

"What is it, Naro?"

"Fiyo, you remember that I was waiting until it seemed safe to have children?"

"Yes. And though it seemed safe at the time, it probably seems less so now, with the Krondir descending on us."

She smiled. "Yes. And safe or not, the time has come. I am expecting your child, Fiyo."

The news stunned him. "My child?"

"Surely you don't think it would be someone else's?" she was laughing at him.

"No, but---. I'd never expected---. When?"

"As near as I can judge, eight months."

He stood there for a while, unable to think of anything else to say. Narolen finally grinned at him and said, "You'd best go on; your men will be wondering about the long delay."

Still half-dazed, he mounted and rode away.

The King of Kings came out to talk to Fatha that morning. Mardrast, unlike his predecessor, did not bother with fancy chariots, but rode a large black horse. He wore armour of gold and silver, trimmed with jewels, and he rode at the head of a bodyguard of twenty heavy cavalry.

As he approached them, Fatha and Vrast both bowed their heads. "Look up," commanded the King of Kings.

They looked up. Mardrast continued to speak. "We need more men. I understand the Krondir are moving south, little by little. I do not wish to wait until they arrive at our gates."

Fatha said nothing, since there was little to be said. The King of Kings continued. "Fatha, will you go out on the Plain and gather in more of your folk?"

Fatha fingered his scarred cheek. "I am not the man to send, Great One. I am an outcast and would almost certainly be killed on sight."

"But you brought back others from the battlefield, others beyond your own small group."

"Yes, Great One, but that was because they recognized it would be better to accompany my band than to flee alone. And it was necessary to issue a special edict once we had arrived to force them to continue to accept my authority."

The King of Kings pounded his fist on his saddle horn. There was a stirring among his bodyguard; the King of Kings was angry with this man in front of him, and perhaps they should immediately arrest him. Or perhaps they should not?

Then the King of Kings was smiling again. "So then. If it must be so, it must be so. Will we be able to win a battle with the Krondir?"

"We can," answered Fatha, "but we will need more troops and we will need commanders who understand the way the Krondir fight."

The King of Kings nodded. "We will have them."

"There is one more thing which might help us."

"And what is that?" The voice was icy. Someone was professing to give unasked-for advice to the King of Kings.

Fatha heard it too, but thought that it would be better to continue than to stop now. "If all or most of the Wanderpeople could have shirts of iron scales, as the heavy cavalry wear, it would help us. They will not stop an arrow that hits squarely, but they do help to prevent wounds; whenever we skirmish with the Krondir, they give us a slight advantage."

The Great One frowned. "Plainsfolk in armour?"

Fatha shrugged. "In order to stop the Krondir, we will need all the advantages we can muster. Armour for the Plainsfolk would be one such."

The King of Kings frowned again. "I doubt if we can provide armour for all, but we can perhaps provide it for a goodly number of them."

"Good."

Humour lightened in the eyes of the King of Kings. "How wonderful to have the approval of an outcast chief of the Plainsfolk! Go on, then, to your work. We will begin delivering the armour as soon as it is ready."

Thus dismissed, Vrast and Fatha went on about their work, and the King of Kings went on to inspect the rest of his troops.

Fatha was awake, but not quite certain what had wakened him. He reached for the sword beside his bed. A sound came faintly to him, almost like the moaning of a wind, but there were words in it. "Fatha, Fatha," it called. He sat up and pulled on his boots.

Narolen was awake now and muttering sleepily, "What is it? What's happening, Fiyo?"

"I don't know, but I intend to find out. Wait here."

The voice was calling again, "Fatha, Fatha," a little louder, but still insistent.

He leaped down from the wagon and looked around. There was no sign of anything or anyone, save for the usual camp-guards. He approached one of them.

"Did you hear anything?"

The other shrugged. "Only the wind, Fatha."

The sound came again, and this time it was nearer. "Fatha, Fatha!"

The guard jerked his head up. "I heard it that time, Fatha. What is it?"

Fatha shrugged. "I don't know, but I don't like it. Do you see anything?"

The man looked around. "Nothing, Fatha."

"Something is making that noise." Fatha saw the look of terror in the man's eyes and turned rapidly.

Where there had been nothing a moment ago, there was now a woman, an old woman, bent and gnarled, in ragged clothes. Her eyes stared at Fatha, stared through him, and there was madness in them.

"Fatha!" she called in a soft moan. He clutched his sword tighter and asked, "What do you want of me?"

She only moaned his name again and tottered toward him on unsteady legs. Despite the apparently infirm legs, she moved quickly. Her outstretched hands almost touched him before he dodged away. He wasn't sure why he dodged, only that something told him to stay away from those withered hands.

She turned to him again. Again, the mad eyes stared through him, at something behind him. She reached for him again, moaning his name. He swung his sword. It passed through her body as through smoke. She hesitated slightly. He dodged again.

The camp-guard sprang on her from behind, grasping her with bare hands, then fell away, slumping to the ground.

Fatha moved, avoiding those grasping hands. He was terrified now, wanting to turn and flee. He knew, though, that running would be futile. Fatha slashed again. Again, the sword passed through the figure before him. Again she hesitated, then came on. The sword was doing something to her, albeit only a little. Could he keep out of reach and keep on swinging until he wore her down?

Again she came at him. Again he moved, swinging the sword. Something whipped past him and through the ancient body. An arrow, he saw. Who had shot it? He had no time to look. She was tottering toward him again. Something else flew by him, a small dart made of some twisted bit of wood. The dart struck her and stayed in the clothing. She staggered forward again, then fell, arms outstretched toward him.

He looked around. Narolen was in the wagon's doorway holding a strung bow in her hands, and Duinifaire was standing a little ways away with another twisted dart ready in his hand.

The little man stepped forward and looked down at her. "The Old Woman!" he muttered.

"You know her?"

The little man smiled slightly. "Not personally. It is that she is one of those beings brought from elsewhere. But it is that she knew who she was seeking."

"Yes, she did. You had no forewarning this time, did you?"

"It is that I had a little warning, but it is that I needed all that time and more to make preparations."

The figure on the ground suddenly became less substantial, lifting off the ground and blowing away like mist in the light breeze of the evening. There was nothing left behind but a slight stink, which also rapidly faded.

Fatha looked down at the guard who had attempted to grapple with the Old Woman. He still breathed, but he was unconscious, and did not look well. Fatha turned to Duinifaire. "Can you do anything for him?"

The little man shook his head doubtfully. "It may be so, it may be not. Let us be seeing."

He knelt down. "What is it that happened to him?"

"When she came at me, he tried to hold her. When he touched her, he fell."

"Ah. It may be, then, there is a chance. Help me carry him to the fire."

They carried him over near to the fire, then set him down and covered him with blankets. Duinifaire went back to his wagon. A little later, he came back with a cup containing some sort of liquid. He lifted the man's head and carefully, patiently, poured it into his mouth, a few drops at a time. By the time he was done there was a small crowd of the outcasts gathered around them, and Fatha heard Narolen explaining to them all what had happened.

After Duinifaire had finished pouring the cup of drink into the unconscious man, Fatha spoke to him. "This was because of the jewel, was it not?"

"It was."

"I heard her from inside my wagon, calling my name, and yet it seemed that no one, not even the camp-guards out in the open, heard her at first."

"It is that she was sent for you in particular. It is that the calling was to get your attention, to cause you to move, that she might discover exactly where you were. So it is that the first calling was for you alone, and few others could hear it."

"Few others? You heard it, then?"

"That is so. And it is as I said that I made preparations as quickly as I could."

"And even so, you were just barely in time. Not in time at all for this poor fellow."

"It is that I am sorry. Sometimes it is that these things happen to the best of us."

"If it were only myself," Fatha said, "I would go right now and toss the jewel back into the lake! But I dare not leave now, for the King of Kings will take it ill and have his revenge on my family."

Duinifaire looked up at him. "Even if you might try," he asked, "is it that you think you would actually live to reach the lake?"

27. The Army Gathers

Time continued to pass, and the Wanderpeople continued to chafe in enforced idleness. True to his promise, the King of Kings began sending out armour to Fatha, who was then responsible for distributing it among the other clans.

Some of them were not happy with the thought of armour, feeling, as Jochon had done at first, that it would make cowards of them. Most of them were eventually brought to realize that the advantages outweighed the disadvantages.

A greater difficulty was the matter of the cattle. The area around the city of Endolashan had already been rather thoroughly grazed during the time before they had marched up to the ill-fated battle. By now, there was practically nothing left.

Fatha sent messages to the city asking permission from the King of Kings for the Wanderpeople to take their cattle out onto the Plain to graze. After a few days and no answer, he sent the same request again. There was still no answer, so on the third day from that, he sent a message informing the King of Kings that the Wanderpeople would be taking their cattle out to the Plains the next day.

When that day came, a hundred heavy cavalry rode out from the city, escorting a rather pale and overweight man, who wore a coat of gold-trimmed armour not as one used to it, but as one who did what was expected of him. Unlike most of the chief men of the Empire he wore no beard, but there was no denying that he was an important person.

Fatha and Vrast went to meet him. He looked at them, a little nervously, as one who has heard tales of the ferocity of these people and is not sure how to tell them something they will not like to hear.

"The King of Kings," he finally announced, "decrees that the people who have come to serve in his army shall not leave the vicinity of the city of Endolashan."

"Ah. And what of our cattle? They are starving."

"The King of Kings decrees that the cattle should be sold in the markets of the city, and that he will see that your people are supplied with food."

"And this would leave my people forever dependent on the good will of the King of Kings. No, our cattle are our fortune, our surety against starvation in the future. We cannot sell them.."

The officer began to look angry. "You refuse the offer of the King of Kings?"

"We do." Fatha forced himself to keep smiling, to speak in a calm and reasonable voice. "Understand, it may indeed be possible for the troops of the King of Kings to force us to do according to his will. But consider, the King of Kings also wishes us to help him fight the Krondir; would he prefer men to fight for him who must be driven to their places in the line of battle by his own heavy cavalry, or men who will fight for him willingly?"

The officer hesitated. "Why not go back and inquire of him," suggested Fatha. "See if he will not indeed allow us to take our cattle out to graze?"

For a moment he thought he might have misjudged the temper of the official, thought that the heavy cavalry were about to be ordered into action. But then the man relaxed, perhaps thinking that he was too much in the forefront, and that his inexperience with weapons and his decorative armour might make him too easy prey if it came to battle.

"I will take your words to the King of Kings. Do nothing until I return."

"So long as you return quickly."

The official shot him an angry look, then turned away.

"They will not love you for that," Vrast said.

"When Mardrast came back from the battle, how many were with him?"

"They say there were twenty heavy cavalry," Vrast answered, looking mystified.

"And when we arrived with the people we had rallied, how long had he been here?"

"Two, three days?"

Fatha nodded. "Just so. I have never mentioned it myself, but I have a feeling that the King of Kings is only waiting for me to bring up the fact that he may have deserted his post as bodyguard to the previous King of Kings, and that I came out of the battle better than he did.

"So long as I never mention it, or even allude to it, he will probably leave me alone, and probably try not to provoke me too greatly.

"But if I should begin making hints about his courage, that will be the time when he will feel it necessary to dispense with my services. And he cannot do so in a way which will cause dissension among my people, for he needs soldiers to fight his war for him."

He thought for a bit, then smiled. "But I will be very careful not to accept invitations to go into the city of Endolashan, and I will be careful to have my camp guarded at night."

"Do you feel that you are in that much danger?"

"No, not so long as I am careful. And so long as I am careful, I am free to press him for things that we need. Even rumours started by Wanderpeople could cause trouble for him with his own people. That, along with the Krondir, could well be too much for him to deal with."

"Only see that you do not press too hard."

"No, nor too often."

Two days later a new edict came out; the herds could be sent off to other pastures, but the wagons must stay. Each clan was allowed to send up to five men out to look after cattle, and two wagons to carry food, supplies, and so on. The remainder were to stay near the city of Endolashan.

28. Foraging

There was a constant coming and going of messengers in and around the city of Endolashan. Those parts of the Empire which had not sent their full contingent to the previous battle were warned to send them now. Those areas which had sent contingents were asked for more.

Rumour even had it that there was a discussion between the King of Dannon-ska and the King of Kings, for the Krondir were spreading out to the west as well as to the south. The King of Jakashan was still living in the city of Endolashan, a pensioner dependent on the King of Kings. He could not do more than gather a small force of heavy cavalry for the previous battle, and only he and ten others had escaped the disaster.

As a result, it was accepted in most quarters that if the Krondir were ever defeated, the King of Jakashan would rule at the pleasure of the ruler of Endolashan.

The season of rains came and went, and the Wanderpeople suffered from sickness. Healers, both from the tribe and from the city, did what they could, but all too often they could do nothing. The Wanderpeople were unused to staying in one place for so long and had little experience in dealing with the diseases that were abroad in the crowded city.

Fatha was not told much about the plans of the Kings, though Vrast was occasionally called into the city to be given fresh orders and information, most of which he would immediately pass on. The King of Kings did not intend to go out to war until he had gathered an army which he felt could defeat the Krondir. Since gathering such an army also involved the feeding of it, and even the arming of a significant part of it, new taxes must be levied, food and other materials bought and stored, and dispensed to the armies as needed.

It was the gathering of the taxes which raised some difficulty, for there was no sense in calling people to the city of Endolashan, only to starve outside the walls while the preparations were made. Messages had to be sent out to deliver the decree requesting the taxes, then officials of the King of Kings had to go out to actually gather the taxes in.

After that, decrees were sent out to require more men to come in to join the King's forces. As well, requests were made to outlying areas to send in quantities of such foodstuffs as were available, and were not likely to spoil easily.

At the request of the King of Kings, Fatha sent or led out scouting parties to the north. The parties went progressively farther until at last they met Krondir scouts scouting southward. It was eventually established that the Krondir held the land within a week's ride northward from Endolashan.

Fatha discussed this situation with Vrast. "They will gradually work their way down to the very walls of Endolashan if nothing is done."

"But we cannot risk a battle until we have gathered all the troops we possibly can."

"No, no, I do not mean to fight a battle! But perhaps some of our Plainsfolk could wander about up there, harass the Krondir, not fighting when there were too many, but raid them, attack small patrols or scouts, let them know that the territory does not belong to them.

"And there might be loot to be had as well; the Great One ought to be grateful for any extra wealth that can be added to his coffers."

Vrast stroked his beard thoughtfully. "I will suggest it. I cannot say what the King of Kings will decide."

A day later, however, word came from the King of Kings to begin just such tactics. The numbers of men to be sent out was to be left to Fatha.

After some consideration, he took a group consisting of half of his own outcasts and half of the other Wanderpeople. He would have preferred to use only his own people, but he knew that to do so would be to cause ill-feeling among the others. Why should Fatha's people have all the opportunity to take loot? On the other hand, to outnumber his own people with the men of other clans was to invite disaster.

The first few days were spent in learning to live together, with both outcasts and Clansmen acting like dogs walking stiff-legged around each other, waiting for the first snarl that would signal the beginning of the fight. Fatha watched them carefully, however, and let it be known that he would exact retribution on any who fought, for whatever cause, or on any who attempted to provoke a fight. The end result was that they managed the affair with only a quarrel or two.

They had some success, though the booty they brought back consisted mostly of Krondir horses and weapons, along with such bits of money or jewelry as they carried with them on patrol.

Fatha next sent out a force comprising a mix of men who had gone out before and men who had not, both outcasts and Clansmen. He sent Jochon out as leader this time, for it was necessary not only to get the other Wanderpeople to accept the outcasts, but to accept orders from them as well. He had little fear of Jochon's ability to instill his authority, perhaps even by the sword if necessary.

It pleased Fatha when the group came back with no such reports, (though it appeared that early on, Jochon had had to knock one rather obstreperous young man out of the saddle). They brought back a little more booty, and the news that the Krondir were now strengthening their forces, making it a little more difficult for small groups to raid them successfully.

29. March to Battle

The rains tapered off, and the Plains were blooming and green again. The army of the King of Kings swelled in size, and those who had been there since the year before became more and more restless, eager to be doing something.

The King of Dannon-ska came riding in with an army numbering several thousand, and joined with these, the army of Endolashan marched northward.

Small groups of the Wanderpeople scouted ahead. Another advantage to the strategy of foraging raids was displayed; the Wanderpeople knew every inch of the ground to the north, knew where bands of Krondir might hide, and were several times able to prevent raids and ambushes. The King of Kings made his pleasure known by distributing a gold coin to each of the men involved.

"All this is very well," Fatha said to Vrast one day, "but we have marched for a long time and have yet to see any sign of the main force of the Krondir."

"Perhaps they are still gathering their troops."

"Perhaps. And yet they have known for some days, perhaps weeks, that we are coming. Surely by now they must have gathered sufficient troops to meet us. Tomorrow we come to the knoll again; one would have thought that they would give battle before then."

"And you suspect some sort of trick or trap?"

"By the toes of the Clan-spirit, I suppose I do! I have a feeling about this, that they are making things too easy for us."

Vrast smiled. "Shall I take that message to the King of Kings for you?"

Fatha smiled in return. "I am sure he would be delighted to know that. No, Vrast my friend, I think I would need more than bad feelings to take to the Great One. I will reorganize my scouts a little, and see if that helps. I have an idea."

He spoke to Jochon a little later. "When we send out scouts, send out more to the flanks. I am wondering if the Krondir are hoping to take us with our backs to the river, where we can maneuver less easily. And I cannot tell this to the King of Kings until I have some proof to show him."

"Very well." Jochon turned away.

"Jochon?"

"Yes?"

"The men of the Clans, are they a little more resigned to taking orders from an outcast now? If we have to give battle tomorrow, for instance, will they accept my commands, or will they take issue with me in the heat of battle?"

Jochon thought on that for a moment. "Most have gotten used to following your orders, and will do so. But you will have to be ready, Fatha. If anyone does object, kill him immediately. You tend to be a little soft-hearted, and in our situation, we cannot afford that. If one objects and is seen to escape unpunished, others may try to do so; then, by the teeth and toes of the Clan-spirit, we will be in trouble."

"Thank you, Jochon, for your honesty."

"Hah! Any answer but the honest one would be poor service to you, Fatha."

The next day, they passed the knoll. Bones still lay on the field, and there were many who shuddered at the sight, considering it an ill omen. The scouts had still found no sight of the Krondir main force.

However, towards evening, one band of scouts came back to report that there were signs of a large band of Krondir off to the west. They had not seen the actual army, only traces where they had passed.

"This we must tell to the King of Kings," Fatha said to Vrast.

"Agreed. I will go immediately."

"And I will strengthen the pickets on the left flank. It is not at all impossible for them to come up during the night and attack in the darkness."

"You think they might?"

"Their best weapon is their archery, coupled with their mobility. I think it unlikely that they will attack when their bows are least useful. But if they think that we might not be expecting them at night, would it not be perhaps their best tactic?"

"But if they think that we think that they will attack by night because they think that we think that they will not attack until day, or if they think that we think that they think---"

"Then we will chase each other's tails around until we end up swallowing ourselves! Stop laughing and go deliver the message."

"I was not laughing, merely smiling a little." Vrast sighed. "I have been working with you Plainsfolk too long; my sense of humour has become like yours."

Fatha went to find Narolen. She was at the campfire, mending a shirt, and she looked up as he approached. "Well?"

"Well enough," he answered. "If there is no battle tomorrow, I will be surprised."

"You have found the Krondir, then?"

"We have found where they have been. Tomorrow morning, they will come whooping out of the west at us."

"Ah. And we are in trouble again?"

"Perhaps not. If the Great One has learned anything from the last battle, we might well win. At any rate, I have learned something from the last battle, and I will at the very least be able to save more troops than last time if the battle breaks down."

She wrapped her arms around her swollen abdomen. "Whatever you do, be sure that you bring yourself safe out of the battle. I would bring your child up fatherless."

He looked at her with concern. "The time is near?"

"Near, but not today nor tomorrow. Do you have anything further to do tonight?"

"No, unless someone comes in suddenly to report that the Krondir are upon us. And I doubt it would be possible, otherwise the scouts would have seen them today. Why do you ask?"

"If you have nothing else to be done, would you sit with me for a while, then?" She smiled a wry smile. "Sometimes I almost miss the times when we were wandering the Great Mother Plain alone, with only each other for company. We are safer from enemies now, but we have less time for each other."

Fatha grimaced. "That is true. And yet--
-"

"No, you need not explain. I understand. In exchange for our safety, something must be given up. Well, it might be worse."

"It might indeed."

Fatha was wakened early in the morning by Jochon. "Fatha, our pickets have been reporting movement all along the west side. Given that much movement, I would suspect that the whole Krondir army is out there."

Fatha shook his head once to clear the sleep out, took in what Jochon had just said, and answered, "Yes, that seems most likely. Send someone to find Vrast."

Inwardly, he cursed the situation which forced him to send and receive all messages through Vrast. Not that he had anything against the man, but it slowed things down considerably. It mattered little so long as they had a good deal of time, but in a battle, time might well be all-important, and who knew what might happen in the delay between sending and receiving of messages?

"Already done, Fatha."

Fatha grinned. "Well, then. If that has already been done, what need have you of me? Why not let me sleep through the battle?"

"What? And have to listen to you forever complaining about being deprived of your part in the defeat of the Krondir?"

Vrast was there very shortly, and had the situation explained to him. "So you want me to go and explain to the King of Kings that we strongly suspect that the enemy are lining up for battle on our right flank, and that we had best move ourselves into position even though it is the middle of the night?"

"Yes."

Vrast smiled slightly. "I hope for all our sakes that you are right. The Great One is not going to appreciate this at all, and if dawn finds no Krondir waiting to attack, he will be very put out."

"And if dawn finds the Krondir ready to overrun us and we are not ready, he will be even more put out, I think."

"That is true. What do you plan to do while I go take my life into my hands?"

"We will have all our Plainsfolk awake and on horseback, taking our place on the left flank of the line."

Darkness shaded into dawn, and with the dawn could be seen the shapes of the Krondir army in a large semicircular formation half-surrounding the Endolashan army. On the other hand, it could be seen that the Krondir line was very thin, and that they intended the semicircular formation more for its effect on the morale of the Endolashan troops than for any serious tactical purpose.

As dawn came up, Fatha had some of his men ride back to the camp and pick up food and water, to be parcelled out among those waiting in line. "There is no sense in having the men go into battle hungry as well as tired," he told Vrast.

"So long as the enemy allows your men time to eat."

Fatha shrugged. "If they do not, we are not that much worse off."

Now, in the rising light, he surveyed his own troops. Only a little more than a half of them were supplied with metal armour, and it had taken his constant efforts and complaints to manage that. There had been constant delays and excuses after about one quarter of the necessary armour shirts were supplied. On the other hand, having quickly seen how things were going, he had had most of the others produce armour of horn plates such as he and his men had worn previously.

He was sure that none of the Clans were happy with the thought of being led by an outcast. Most would follow orders up to the point when they saw an obvious chance to escape both him and the vengeance of the King of Kings, and he thought he could manage with that.

A horn sounded far off on the right flank of the Endolashan army, and was taken up by horns in the various contingents of the army along its length. With no further order from Fatha, the Wanderpeople advanced. He looked over to the left; yes, the leftmost section of the line was holding back, preparing to face the Krondir if they should come in from the flank.

Suddenly the Krondir were moving. Almost from a standing start, their horses were galloping towards the Endolashan army, and they were readying their bows.

Fatha shouted a word of command, and the Plainsfolk galloped as well, bringing up their own bows. Arrows criss-crossed in the air, men fell, the charges continued. There was time for one more flight of arrows each, then they were in contact.

The din of men shouting, horses screaming, swords clanging seemed to go on forever. Suddenly, a piercing whistle sounded from the Krondir side, and a moment later, they were fleeing. Fatha noticed that there was a bright score across the iron plates on his chest, but he could not remember having taken the blow. He had barely any time to realize that the iron shirt had saved his life before he had to call his men back from pursuit.

Some were not recalled; a few of the men of the Clans, having apparently forgotten the lessons of plains warfare, continued the pursuit, heedless of orders. Nothing could be done about them.

Fatha looked around; the Krondir were still pressing the left flank, trying to overwhelm the small force facing them. He took much of his troops and swung them around to strike the flank of the enemy. Almost too late, the Krondir saw them coming and fled. A few of them were slow getting away and were caught and killed, then Fatha had to get his men organized before the main body came back again.

And back they came. This time they attacked in short little rushes, loosing arrows and fleeing before they came to grips. It was a style of fighting which would have had better effect against other enemies, for the Wanderpeople were also bowmen, and quite able to exchange arrow for arrow.

Fatha had had his people spread out a little, so as not to present a solid target for the Krondir arrows. It helped, but they still lost men in each rush.

But the Krondir were also losing men in each rush, and the Wanderpeople showed no sign of breaking ranks to pursue them, so the Krondir tactic was unsuccessful.

The Krondir held back in a solid body for a while, then. Fatha looked to the right, but there was too much dust down there to say what was happening. He could ride down, or send a man down to find out, but there was not likely to be time to affect the outcome of that battle; he would have to win his own little battle by himself.

The Krondir were coming back again now, in a massive charge. They might hope to overwhelm the Wanderpeople thus, but the armour of the Plainsfolk gave them a minor advantage at close quarters. Arrows flew again, then the two forces clashed. The Krondir were set on crushing them this time.

30. Victory!

Again, there was the swirling, noisy, dusty confusion of hand-to-hand cavalry fighting. Not much of it stayed in Fatha's memory, save a vague sense of hacking at snarling yellow faces, and once a sword-cut that was coming at his unprotected side before another sword cut off the threatening arm. He half turned to see Jochon beside him, a grim smile on his face. Then the battle closed round them again.

Suddenly, the Krondir were fleeing again. They were brave men, skilled in fighting, but the advantage of the armour lay with the Wanderpeople. Slowly, that advantage had begun to tell, and eventually the Krondir could take no more. Fatha brought his men after them, loosing arrows at them as they went, waiting for them to rally.

This time, however, they did not rally. Fatha realized he was far from the battlefield, and that anything might happen on the right wing. He rallied the men who were close around him, and sent messengers to rally whoever might be gathered of the rest of the Wanderpeople, then rode back.

Not all of them could be rallied, though most still followed Fatha's orders; he brought them back to the battlefield to find the other wing of the Endolashan army being hard-pressed by the rest of the Krondir.

He charged his men into the rear of the Krondir, catching them practically unawares, though they were disengaging when his charge hit. Shortly after that, the battle was over.

The King of Kings had been in the thick of the fighting. His bodyguard had ridden with him, of course, and had done their best to protect him, but he was no man to sit in a golden chariot and watch other men doing his fighting.

He had taken a few blows himself, and his sword-arm, as with any swordsman being the most exposed portion of his body, showed one large cut and numerous lesser nicks. Fatha approached him, lowering his head as he came.

"Come forward, Chief of the Plainsfolk, and report!" His voice was full of good humour.

Fatha looked up. "We have defeated them, O King of Kings. Their army is scattered and driven from the field, and they have suffered great losses."

"Hah!" The dark eyes flashed with delight. "They are completely destroyed?"

"No, Great One, but if we continue to march and push them back, they will not be able to gather short of Jakashan, and perhaps not even there.”

“How soon can we march?” It was clear that the King of Kings would be willing to begin marching that very day, in fact, that very minute.

Fatha looked up at the sky, and was amazed to find that it was barely noon. “O Great One, you could probably find a few thousand who would be ready and willing to go immediately. If we stop to eat and care for the wounded, some of us might begin marching this afternoon. On the whole, it might be better to spend the night here and march in the morning.”

“And allow the enemy the night to rally themselves?” There was a strange light in the eyes of the King of Kings.

“O Great One, they are scattered, and we are still whole. Surely they may use the night to rally, but think how much better state we shall be in, for we shall use the night to rest, to care for our wounded, to have a good breakfast, and then be out chasing them. And to be sure that they do not all rally during the night, we can set some of our cavalry to pursuing and harrying them.”

The King of Kings sat for a moment frowning at Fatha, then spoke. “So be it. I give you charge of this pursuit and harrying, since your men are the better suited to it.”

“At your command, O King of Kings.”

31. Grannon

Three weeks later, Fatha was leading his men back to the camp. They had been harrying the Krondir, chivvying them northward up the road ever since the battle, and had prevented them from rallying.

They had been constantly on the move, riding, raiding, living in rough camps at night, returning to the wagons of the main force from time to time to replenish their supply of food or to get new arrows. This time, however, Fatha had important news for the King of Kings, and he rode to tell it.

Vrast was with him, as Vrast had been with them for all the last few weeks, riding as hard and living as uncomfortably as any nomad, and not complaining. He had earned the respect of the Wanderpeople, though even he admitted he was not near to being so accomplished a bowman as any of them.

The officials who regulated access to the King of Kings were not inclined to allow two such filthy and bedraggled specimens to come before his presence, and had suggested to them they come back in the morning.

Vrast, however, was not willing to stand still for any such thing. "We bring news for the King of Kings. If we come back tomorrow, and he asks us why we did not see him immediately after we arrived, what will you tell him? Go on, fools, for you are treading near to doom!"

At this, the officials decided it would indeed be possible for the two to see the King of Kings, but only for a moment, and woe to them if their news was not as important as they claimed.

The King of Kings was relaxing, wearing a long purple robe and a crown. A replica of that worn by his predecessor, the old crown had probably ended up as loot for some Krondir warrior. The King of Kings had also been drinking wine, though only to the point where his eyes were a little brighter than usual.

"Ah, my loyal servant Vrast and the Chief of the Plainsfolk! You have news, I understand?"

"Yes, O Great One," Fatha answered. "The Krondir are preparing to give battle again. We harried and harassed them as much as we could, and delayed their gathering, but we could not halt it. Tomorrow they will fight again."

"Tomorrow?"

"Tomorrow, Great One."

"How many?"

"Perhaps as many as last time, though they have had to call in their clans from all across the land to produce so large a force."

"Hah! So now we face them, and defeat them!"

"Yes, O Great One."

The eyes of the King of Kings narrowed. "You do not seem so confident, Chief of the Wanderpeople. Do you doubt our ability?"

Fatha brought himself erect. "No, O Great One. It is only that I am weary. As for defeating them, we can do that, but it will not be easy at all."

"You think not?" There were signs of danger in the eyes of the King of Kings.

Vrast interrupted smoothly here. "O Great One, all that the Chief of the Plainsfolk means is that we will have to fight, and fight hard, for the Krondir have very little room to retreat. They are cornered, and will therefore fight the harder for it. That is all."

"Oh." The Great One waved a hand dismissively. "Well, we shall prepare to fight tomorrow. On the way out, tell them to send for the messengers; we must send word immediately for all our contingents to be ready to fight tomorrow."

As Fatha and Vrast rode through the encampment of the Wanderpeople, Fatha could sense that something was afoot. People looked at him, and the look was as if they knew a secret he did not know. He was beginning to wonder whether some other Clan chief had taken advantage of his absence to take control of all the Clans, but whatever the secret was, it seemed more a matter of merriment than a threat.

As he neared his own wagon, he saw the looks were more and more accompanied by smiles, and this made him wonder all the more. When he finally reached his own wagon, a woman from one of the clans was tending the fire and cooking, and there was no sign of Narolen. Temo was beside the wagon, and when he saw Fatha riding up, he stuck his head inside and said something that was not audible to those outside.

He then came over to hold the horses for Vrast and Fatha as they dismounted, then to take the horses and see to unsaddling them and putting them out to graze. A moment later, Narolen came out of the wagon carrying a baby in her arms.

He was so tired that for a moment he didn't quite realize what this meant, then suddenly he rushed forward. "Our child, Naro? When?"

"He was born yesterday morning. He is very healthy, as you can see, although he spends most of his time sleeping."

"And you? You are well, Naro?"

"Very well. Still a little tired, but well. We have been waiting for you to come so we can give him a name."

"Ah, a name." He was quiet, then laughed with embarrassment. "All my wits have flown away. I cannot think of names at all."

"Why not Grannon?"

"Grannon?" He was still for a moment. Grannon! The name brought back memories, memories of his father, the strong man on the horse, the man who taught him patiently how to live on the Great Mother Plain, who had told his wide-eyed son tales of the bright realms of the Other People, the tricks of the Grass People. This brought him also to the memory of Grannon with an arrow in his chest, Grannon dying in the wagon and being buried. And further, to the manipulation of Bougil and Yopan, to the sound of his own Clan shouting for him to be cast out.

He shook himself. Why should the bad memories outweigh the good? Yes, call the boy Grannon, in memory of what his father had been for him!

"A very good idea! Grannon he shall be, then!"

All of this led to a celebration, then, for the naming of a child of the Wanderpeople was always a joyful occasion.

For a time, Vrast stood by with a look of mild disapproval on his face. Finally, he approached Fatha. "We will fight a battle tomorrow. Is it wise to spend this night celebrating?"

Fatha smiled. "How can I deny them this time of joy? In particular because, as you say, there will be a battle tomorrow; for how many of them will this be the last chance for enjoyment?"

So they celebrated that night, and in the morning they were formed up in their position on the left flank of the army facing the Krondir.

32. Etiar

The battle before Jakashan was long and hard-fought. Through most of the day, the nomads tried to avoid coming to grips with the Endolashan army, but instead made many quick advances and retreats, loosing showers of arrows, always hoping to draw the army of the King of Kings into an unwise attack.

They generally avoided the left wing, where the skill of the Wanderpeople at mounted archery and mobile warfare was near the equal of their own, but concentrated mainly on the infantry troops of the centre, and the heavy cavalry, who were without missile weapons.

But the men of Endolashan had learned as well. They were in an open formation which did not present a massed target for the Krondir arrows. When the Krondir advanced, the infantry crouched down to present even smaller targets. Bodies of foot archers were posted behind the lines, and they marched to support whatever part of the line might be under Krondir attack.

For Fatha and the Wanderpeople, the battle consisted mostly of sitting quietly and waiting for something to happen. Occasionally, the Krondir attacked their section, but never drew them into a counter-attack.

It was the intention of the King of Kings to stand fast while the Krondir wore themselves out with their dash-and-retire tactics, then advance toward them, keeping the army together, and eventually to drive the nomads from the field. Once they scattered in retreat, then they might be pursued.

However, as the day wore on, Fatha took advantage of the fact that the Krondir were ignoring his force. He chose a group of his men, and when the Krondir rode forward to shoot at the infantry, he sent this group out to shoot into the Krondir flank.

The Krondir were caught by surprise and very nearly stampeded into a rout. Then a force of Krondir rode rapidly out in the hopes of catching and destroying the small detachment of Wanderpeople. Fatha ordered the bulk of his people to counter-attack, and there was a short but vicious cavalry battle.

Some of the Krondir had taken to wearing armour of horn plates such as Fatha and his men had used, but there were not enough of these to make a real difference. It was the Krondir who finally withdrew, though they were by no means broken.

A little later, when the King of Kings had decided that the enemy was sufficiently tired, he ordered his general advance. The Krondir, who had already tired themselves in fruitless raids, continued to ride out and harass the advance, but Fatha sent several small troops of his men down to advance before the infantry, and thus to weaken the effect of the Krondir tactics.

The Krondir also sent small parties around to harass the flanks of the Endolashan army. On Fatha's flank, a screen of mounted archers prevented them from doing much damage.

The Krondir never came into contact with any large portion of the Endolashan army. They backed away, loosing arrows, and when the main body of the Wanderpeople were within range of them, the retreat became a little quicker. After the Endolashan advance had gone on for several hours, the Krondir were losing organization, and some small groups were retreating and fleeing independently.

Even then, it took some more time before the battle ended, and again it was the Wanderpeople who saw to it that the retreat continued, that the Krondir had no time to rally.

For a week and more they harried the Krondir northward, and this time it was not only Krondir warriors that they harried, but trains of carts bearing Krondir families. Fatha remembered the wagons of the Plainsfolk which had been destroyed by the Krondir, but even that memory could not make his heart so hard against the northern nomads as some.

Some of the worst atrocities were carried out by the heavy cavalry of Endolashan, who were not content with giving a quick death to Krondir in their path, but delighted in torture and destruction. It did not take long for Fatha to become heartily sick of this sort of war.

There came an afternoon when they had passed three distinct masses of smoking ruin where the heavy cavalry had passed. In each case, there were always one or two left alive, alive but so badly used by the Endolashan warriors that they had no hope of survival. In each case, the Plainsfolk killed them out of mercy.

In the last instance, they had caught the nomad carts in the same place where some Krondir had long ago caught a small group of Plainsfolk wagons. Fatha gestured at a weathered ruin of a burned-out wagon, and then at the remnants of the Krondir. "This is vengeance, I suppose."

Jochon, who was at his side as usual, shook his head. "This is merely men acting as animals. Vengeance requires that you cause the person who did wrong to suffer."

Fatha looked around. "We have done enough. We will ride to the top of that rise, and if we see no Krondir warriors from there, we turn back."

Jochon said nothing.

They came to the top of the rise, and there below them in a spread-out line was a train of Krondir carts. They numbered about fifty warriors, and Fatha could almost feel the desperation in them as they sought to flee the destruction that had come upon their people. Even as he watched, one of them looked up at the rise and pointed to the Wanderpeople.

Fatha turned to his men. "There has been enough of fighting and of slaying. Stay here unless you are needed. Jochon, will you come with me to talk to them?"

"If you wish it," answered Jochon, though he sounded none too enthusiastic.

"How will we know if we are needed?" asked a young warrior.

Fatha smiled. "You will know, believe me."

The Krondir warriors came now to make a screen in front of their families. They watched as Fatha and Jochon rode down, and though each of the Krondir had an arrow nocked on his string, they held their bows down by their sides.

Their leader was a small man, and young, as near as Fatha could judge Krondir ages. He had, somehow or other, achieved a fair command of the language of the Wanderpeople, though when he could not find a word in that tongue, he quite readily tossed in a word of his own language.

"If you come to destroy us, Plainsman, some of you will die first."

"If I came to destroy you, my men and I would have ridden down and destroyed you."

"So? You do well to be afraid. Even small numbers of us can kill many before we are overwhelmed."

Fatha smiled, but shook his head. "It is nothing to do with fear. It is a matter of having seen altogether too much of slaying and being slain."

"There are other choices for us? My kind are enemies of your kind, and when we find each other, we fight and we kill and we die.”

“Look, young fool, I am trying to find another choice for us,” Even as he said that, Fatha realized the other was hardly younger than he himself. “If we attack each other, what good will come of it? My men are numerous enough to defeat yours, and what happens to your families then? You can protect them while you are alive, but when you are dead, what then?”

“And if we do not fight and die, what then? Are we to become your slaves?”

“No.” Fatha was working out his plans as he went along. “You will come back as prisoners, but not as slaves. And you will be prisoners of the Wanderpeople, not of the King of Kings of Endolashan.”

He saw the young man pulling himself erect with a pride which dared not admit defeat. In a moment, this young chief was going to give a command to his warriors, and even though Fatha and Jochon might die immediately, the young Krondir and his people would die soon after.

He touched his hand to his cheek. “Do you know enough about the Wanderpeople to know what these scars mean? They mean I am an outcast. I was cast out of my Clan, put out on my own, with my woman, my wagon, and my horse. There was no life left for me save to wander the Great Mother Plain until I died, either naturally or by being killed by anyone who found me.

“But I had a woman with me, as I said. I would have let myself starve, but she convinced me that was a coward's way. It was more difficult to live, but it required me to do things I had never thought of, to be mere than just a mere wanderer of the plains.

"You have families with you. You see it a shame to let yourselves be called prisoners. But perhaps it would be better to be prisoners than to be dead, and leave your wives and families prey to whoever should come along."

"Prisoners? What would that mean? Slaves?"

"No, I have told you that you would not be slaves. You would be subject to my command, but I will promise you here and now that I will treat you as my own people."

As he made this promise, Fatha realized that there might come a time when the King of Kings would ask him what right he had to give such promises. But that was for the future.

"You promise that no harm shall come to us?"

"Insofar as it is in my ability to do so, I shall see that no harm comes to you."

The Krondir thought carefully, then spoke to his fellows, in his own language. There followed some heated discussion, and it was clear that not all of those present were in favour of agreeing to Fatha's proposition. There was a time or two when he was almost certain that one of the warriors was going to end the argument by letting fly an arrow, but in the end, the young leader prevailed.

"We are your prisoners, then. What is your name?"

"I am Fatha, and this is Jochon. And you?"

"My name is Etiar."

33. The Warriors

They rode back to Jakashan only to find that the King of Kings had taken most of his army and returned to Endolashan. The King of Jakashan was once more installed in his city, but his authority was very limited. He was only allowed to raise troops with the permission of the King of Kings and was allowed only a limited number of troops under his command. To ensure that he did not transgress any of these restrictions, he was required to have in his court certain ambassadors and advisors appointed by the King of Kings.

The King of Kings had even ordered that the wagons of the Wanderpeople should return to Endolashan, the main reason given was that there was little enough food to be found near Jakashan, and that it was best for the families of the Wanderpeople to return to their herds at Endolashan.

Vrast also rejoined them at Jakashan. He was pleased to be with Fatha again, though he never said so in so many words. When he saw the Krondir, however, he frowned.

"Who are these?"

"They are prisoners. Their leader's name is Etiar."

"Prisoners? Whoever ordered the taking of prisoners?"

"No one. We decided this on our own."

Vrast frowned. "The King of Kings may not be happy about this."

Fatha shrugged. "The Krondir are defeated. What reason would he have for being unhappy?"

"You intend to turn them over to him?"

"No. I have no intention of even telling him they exist unless he asks. And I doubt that he will ask, unless someone brings it to his attention."

"Leaving me in the position of either betraying my King by not informing him, or betraying you by informing him? Not a happy choice, Fatha."

"Why talk of betrayal? By the teeth and toes of the Clan-spirit, what have we here? About fifty warriors and their families? Are they about to overrun the land and conquer Endolashan? I have brought them with me, and I will be responsible for them."

They continued along the way to Endolashan. They were still three days out of the city and thinking to find a place to camp for the night, when they suddenly came upon Duinifaire and his wagon. Fatha had a sudden premonition of danger. He rode forward to greet the little man.

"Ah, Duinifaire! A good day to you. And what brings you out here?"

"Ah, Fatha! A good day to you also. And is it that you cannot truly guess what brings me out here?"

"I hoped I was wrong."

Duinifaire shook his head. "Unfortunately, it is that there has been another warning, and I thought it would be best to be with you until the danger passes."

"I see."

"And there is one other thing, Fatha."

"Yes?"

"You recall that Nik-Malo promised you advice in return for the service that you are doing her? It is that you ought to be wary of the King of Kings. During his time of need, he might be grateful and appreciative; now that it has come time to pay you for your service, it is that he may be less so."

Fatha considered that for a bit, then nodded. "I did expect him to be as loyal to me as I was to him, though perhaps I ought to have known better. Thank you, Duinifaire, I will be watchful. Now as to this other danger...?"

"You remember the Hounds that were called into this world from another? And likewise the Old Woman? It is that there is another world from which Warriors may be called. It is that a single Warrior would probably be enough against one unprotected. He would be brought into this world at an arm's distance from you, strike, and be gone before you realized you were dead.

"But it is that it is not so easy for our enemy, thanks to the protection I offer. First, it is that I can keep most of them from coming at all. Second, I can prevent them from coming quite so quickly, and see that they do not come without warning.

"When it is that you hear the sound of a chime, at that moment look all around you; somewhere near to you will be a gleaming cloud, and in the next instant the Warrior will step forth from that. It is that you must be ready to strike before he is. You had best also warn those men nearest to you that they may also be on guard."

"How long have you known about this?"

"Since this morning."

"This morning? And you are here already? How?"

Duinifaire shook his head. "If I am here to protect you from these things, then it must be that I have powers to deal with them, and if it is that I have such powers, then what is so surprising about my being here? Certainly nothing more surprising than that my wagon just happened to break down exactly in your path out there on the Plain?"

"No, I suppose not. It is a little frightening, perhaps."

"Perhaps. But think of it this way: These powers of mine are being used to the end of keeping you alive."

"Yes, I suppose so." Fatha turned away, then something occurred to him and he turned again. "What of Narolen and the babe? Are they well?"

Duinifaire grinned. “Quite well. It is that the child is healthy and growing; Narolen is healthy as well, though a little pressed, what with all the usual work and the babe as well. No, do not worry about them, Fatha.”

With Duinifaire’s warning in his mind, Fatha was expecting an attack at any moment. None came during that night, nor during the next day.

The night after, as they were sitting around the campfires engaging in the usual evening talk of men of war at evening campfires, there was the sound of a chime.

Fatha was caught by surprise, and it was another instant before he connected that sound to the warning of Duinifaire. He surged to his feet, reaching for his sword, looking all around him. He saw his men still sitting there, dumfounded, though Jochon was moving even as Fatha looked at him.

There was a faint, nacreous glow in the air off to his right. His sword was still leaving the sheath when out of the glow came a tall, slender figure leaping toward him.

He had only an instant to take it in as the warrior came; it was taller than himself by a good two palm-breadths, though it was slimmer by at least as much, even at the chest. The warrior wore what appeared to be a kilt of very pale leather at the middle, along with a breastplate of leather with a pair of black metal plates fastened to it. On its head was a helmet of black metal, bearing a crest of some reddish fur. The feet were unshod, the arms and hands bare, though covered with thick short hair. The right arm was upraised, before it struck down with a narrow curved scimitar.

The face under the helm was the face of a wolf with a short muzzle. It had large yellow eyes, wide black nostrils, and it let out a snarling yell, displaying a fearsome set of wolf-like teeth.

Fatha had barely time to react, bringing up his own sword in a parry so late that he almost felt the scimitar on his head. As the other's stroke went past, Fatha brought his sword up and around in a quick circle to chop into the armoured side. So fierce and strong was his own blow that the wolf-warrior was flung aside, landing in a sprawl which forced the other warriors of Fatha's band to fling themselves aside to avoid the flying corpse.

The wolf-warrior lay there, and Fatha stepped over to look at him more closely, but even as he moved, the pale cloud covered the body, and it disappeared.

Fatha looked around. Jochon was standing, sword in hand. A few of the others had weapons out as well, and all were staring at him. He forced himself to smile and shrugged. "I have enemies," he said.

They were still not entirely satisfied. He saw Duinifaire stumping up the hill into the firelight. "I have friends as well," he said. He looked around at them again. Something more needed to be said.

"Some time back, I made a promise. I gave my word as part of a bargain, and I promised to hold something for someone. I am required to defend the thing I hold from time to time. And you may have wondered why Duinifaire joined his wagon to ours; that was because it was recognized that I would need some assistance, for I know less of magic than I know what keeps the stars from falling to earth.

"And you need not fear, any of you. It is me they seek, not you. If sometime Duinifaire's magic fails, it is only myself that will die, and not you. I will understand, of course, if you fear riding too near to me from now on."

That settled it. They might fear and distrust magic. They might even wish to put a good deal of distance between themselves and this man who was being magically hunted. But suggest that this was an admission of fear and they could not flee, not unless they wished to be surrounded by devils.

A little later, Duinifaire took Fatha aside. "Be careful, Fatha. It is that I have been able to slow their attacks and give you warning, but there are still other things that they could do. For instance, it is that they might attempt to send a dozen or so against you at one time. My protection can even hinder that, to some degree, but it may not be able to prevent it entirely."

Fatha shrugged. "Well, we will face what we will face when we face it. Thank you for your concern."

The little man smiled. "It is that I was sent to do a job, Fatha, but I have come to rather like your company. It would be a shame to lose you now."

There were no further attacks that night. In the morning, however, as they were saddling up to leave, the warning chime sounded again. Fatha was better-prepared this time; his sword was already in his hand, and when the Warrior leaped through the pale cloud, swinging his sword in a waist-level stroke, Fatha blocked it with his own weapon immediately. At the same instant, Jochon stepped in to thrust once, accurately.

The next attack did not come until evening again. Once more, as they were seated around the campfire, the warning chime sounded. It was barely dying away when it sounded again, and again, seeming to go on and on. Fatha was uncertain, but he felt that there must have been thirty chimes or more.

Then he was fencing with the first of the Warriors. For all his tallness, the Warrior was very light, and thus his blows had less force behind them. Fatha could finally get inside his guard and, having put him down, looked around for the next foe.

All around him was a struggling mass of his own people and the Warriors, with more still arriving. The Warriors all had Fatha as a target and tried to go past anyone else; several of them had died ignoring armed men. They only engaged others of the Wanderpeople if there was no way to get past them to Fatha.

Jochon kept two of them busy, by moving quickly enough that they could never quite disengage from him. Fatha stepped in and struck at one of them, leaving Jochon free to deal with the other.

It was still a busy time. Amid the combat, Fatha recalled seeing Duinifaire swinging his own double axe with fearsome effect.

Then, almost as suddenly as they had come, they were gone. Fatha looked around. Some of his men had taken wounds, mostly mere nicks and scratches, though a couple were more seriously hurt. He took Duinifaire aside.

"How often will this happen?"

The little man shrugged. "Probably not again, now that it is shown to be ineffective. It is that they may try once or twice more singly, hoping that they may catch you by surprise, but other than that, probably not again."

Twice the next day there was the sound of the chime and a Warrior came rushing out of a pearly cloud to attack Fatha. Neither attack was successful, though they caused the men of Fatha's band to become very wary.

They arrived at last at Endolashan and went to find their own wagons and families. The Krondir under Etiar moved in to camp near to Fatha's group of outcasts; it had been his promise which had brought them to surrender, and they did not yet trust the other Wanderpeople completely.

No sooner had Fatha unsaddled his horse when a rider, all splendid in red and gold, came to him, a messenger from the King of Kings. "The King of Kings requires from you a report of your actions. He will meet you at the City Gate at the second hour after sunrise."

34. Wages of the King of Kings

The King of Kings was clearly not happy. Fatha wondered at that; the Krondir were destroyed and scattered. What more did he want? Small bands of the Krondir might indeed live a bandit existence around the fringes of the Empire, but they were no longer a threat to the King of Kings.

He waited for the Great One to speak.

"Are the Krondir destroyed, then, that you have returned already?"

"The Krondir will be no threat to you or your Kingdom for years to come, O King of Kings."

"I would have them destroyed to the last."

Fatha almost shrugged, but kept himself from doing so. The King of Kings was a powerful man. "They will be no trouble to you, O Great One, not for many years."

But the King of Kings was not to be mollified. "They were to be destroyed! Did they not endanger my very life? They should be wiped out, and you ought to have seen to that before you returned from the field! Are you all cowards, then or disloyal?"

"As to that, O King of Kings, your own heavy cavalry are quite brave enough to see to the massacre of women and children. We agreed to be soldiers, not murderers." Even as he spoke, Fatha realized he was speaking unwisely.

The face of the King of Kings was white, and Fatha saw that there were some in his entourage who understood the language of the Wanderpeople, for there were other white faces as well. Fatha spoke again, hoping to mollify the Great One. "The Krondir are destroyed, O Great One. The war is over. We could indeed ride out again after them, but even if we caught them, what then? They are beyond your borders and still fleeing, and I doubt that they will come back. And my men have not seen their own families for a long while. Give us a few days' rest, and if you still will it, we will ride out again."

There was a moment when he knew that all hung in the balance, that the Great One was on the point of ordering him to be slain. But then the Lord of Endolashan calmed himself and smiled, a very small smile.

"No, you my well be right. Go to your wives and families. We will begin to gather your pay for you, and it should be delivered in a few days. You may go."

As they rode back to the wagons, Jochon spoke quietly. "He does not like you, Fatha. And you upset him by talking so to him."

"Yes, I know. I was a little careless, Jochon, and let him push me into saying things that ought not to have been said. And there is more. You recall that he said that he would begin gathering our pay? I wonder if he will not begin thinking of ways to avoid paying us?"

"Such as what?"

"Ah, that I am not sure. Still, Jochon, will you go around to the Clans and tell them to be wary? Set out guards at night, keep the horses near the wagons, that sort of thing?"

"Of course."

When Fatha returned to his wagon, he found a small group of men there, all of them leaders of small Clans. He looked around at them and saw embarrassment on all their faces.

One of them finally stepped forward. "Ah, Fatha!"

"Ah, Lomon! How may I help you?"

"This fighting, Fatha. It has taken many of our men. All of our Clans were small before; now we number no more than ten to fifteen warriors, with many widows and orphans. You know what sort of fate we can expect on the Plain? The larger clans will destroy us."

"Ah." Fatha nodded.

"We might even gather together, and we would form a group of almost sufficient size. But some of the larger Clans would still be willing to attack us for the sake of our cattle. What we ask, then, is that you allow us to join with you, for protection."

"There are some other Clans here of about the same size as my band. Have you not talked to them?"

"Three of them. They all set conditions for joining them, conditions which would make us no more than beggars among them."

"And what conditions would you accept from me?"

This surprised them a little, for they expected that as petitioners, they would negotiate from conditions set by Fatha. Such conditions usually had much to do with the status of the petitioners within the new group, and that status could vary anywhere from equal partners to utter subservience.

After a moment, Lomon began to state conditions, trying hard to strike a balance, not so high that Fatha would reject them out of hand, nor so low that they could not allow themselves to be bargained down.

Fatha, on the other hand, was only too glad that they could not read his mind and know how much he wanted to have them join. And he could not make the conditions too light, either, lest they begin to feel that he was belittling them. In the end, they came to an arrangement acceptable to both sides.

Three days later, the King of Kings sent a wagon out to them, a wagon laden with gold. The officer leading the escort brought the wagon to Fatha, and pronounced loudly, "The King of Kings pays those who have served loyally!"

He was about to turn and ride away when Fatha said, "A moment, fellow!"

Not used to being addressed so, the officer whirled, his hand moving to his sword.

"Peace, peace! I only meant that we ought to see that the count is correct before you leave."

"That is the business of the scribes!"

Fatha shrugged. "If you say so."

But the officer waited until the money had been counted out. There was approximately half of what had been promised. The scribe, a tall gangling man with a skimpy beard, was somewhat embarrassed. Fatha could guess what had happened; the scribe had been told that the Plainsfolk would be too thrilled to be receiving any gold at all to be concerned about how much there was, if indeed they could count. He now found himself in the position of having to insist that he had brought full payment when everyone knew that he had not.

He tried to bluff it out at first. "You are now fully paid for services done for the King of Kings," he announced.

Fatha shook his head. "No, barely half paid."

The scribe stuck out his chin. "You are saying that my count was wrong?"

"No, your count was quite correct. Only that the gold you have brought is barely half what the King of Kings promised us."

"Then you are saying that the King of Kings is breaking his promise."

"How would I know? All I know is that the money here is not what we were promised."

"You had best not press this claim. The King of Kings will not take kindly to having his honesty questioned."

"I question no one's honesty yet. All I say is that we will wait until we are fully paid. Take that word back to your masters."

The scribe unsuccessfully tried to stare Fatha down, then wheeled the wagon round and drove back to the city.

Fatha sent messengers to all the Clans of the Wanderpeople that they should come and receive the first payment from the King of Kings. Each of the Clan chiefs came separately, and as he gave out the money, Fatha explained the situation. He could see that some doubted his explanation, perhaps suspecting him of holding back the gold. None would actually challenge him over it.

That same day the King of Dannon-ska returned with his cavalry to Endolashan. They had been pursuing the Krondir, and had just finished making their leisurely way back to the presence of the King of Kings.

The next morning a messenger came out from the city to the Wanderpeople. He found Fatha and asked, "Are you the leader of the people of the Plains?"

"I am."

"I bear a message from the King of Kings. He asks, "Why do you linger about my walls? You have received the money promised you, now you may go."

He waited, for it was his duty also to bring back any message that Fatha might wish to send.

Fatha shook his head. "Tell the King of Kings this: 'The money we have received was only half what was promised. We wait for the remainder.'"

The messenger took a moment to ensure that he had the message correct, then turned and galloped away. Fatha and Jochon watched him go. "Worse and worse, Fatha," said Jochon. "I do not think he means to pay us."

Fatha sighed. "You may well be right, Jochon. Well, we will stay here for another two days, then leave. It is unfortunate, but if he decides not to pay us, there is little we can do."

Late that night, Fatha was wakened by the sound of the alarm-horns blowing. Coming out of his bed half-awake, he wondered at first who was raiding the cattle, then even as he was scrambling into his scale-armour shirt, he realized that the cattle were far out on the Plains. He knew what was happening, even without looking; the King of Kings had sent out his troops to attack the encampment of the Wanderpeople.

Narolen was awake now, and Grannon, disturbed by the movement, made a querulous sound. "We are under attack from the city," he told her quickly. "Get ready, get the wagon moving!"

He was outside now. Temo was sliding lithely from the tent beside the wagon. "What is it, Fatha?"

"Attack, Teyo! Hitch up the oxen and get the wagon moving! Don't stop to load up too much, just go!" Fatha noticed even as he was speaking that Temo was no longer the boy they had rescued from the town of Hadar-esh; he was becoming a young man.

Fatha strung his bow and ran for his horse. Off toward the city he could see wagons burning, and even as he looked, another fire bloomed orange in the night. He felt a pang, knowing what the loss of a wagon meant to a Plainsman. He had trusted the King of Kings too much! They ought to have taken their losses and left a day ago.

By the time he had his horse saddled and was riding off to join the other warriors of the Wanderpeople who were riding toward the disturbance, Jochon was by his side. "I think the King of Kings is paying off his debt," said Jochon.

"Exactly my thought. We have to get the wagons moving, save whatever we can. It is good luck for us that our herds are off on the Plains beyond the reach of the King of Kings."

He picked several of the younger men and sent them off to ride through the camps, ordering the people to move the wagons out onto the plains. The rest would have to do what they could to prevent the Endolashan warriors from destroying wagons.

Many of the wagons which had been closest to the walls of the city were now burning. Most of the warriors who had been with those wagons were dead, though some still fought. As they rode, Fatha could see a few figures on foot leaping and dodging among the heavy cavalry and their spears.

As they came nearer, Fatha realized that the attackers were not the Endolashan heavy cavalry, but rather the warriors of Dannon-ska. "Ha! Performing one last service for the King of Kings before he releases them to their own homes!"

"What was that?" asked Jochon, and it was only then that Fatha realized that he had spoken aloud.

"The cavalry of Dannon-ska, doing the work of the King of Kings," said Fatha.

By this time they were in battle, and there was little time for talk. The warriors of the Wanderpeople were growing more numerous on the field all the time, but even so they were not suited to hand-to-hand combat with the heavy cavalry, and at night their archery was not so deadly as by day.

But still they did their best, charging, shooting, harrassing the heavy cavalry as they attacked the wagons. The heavy cavalry, on the other hand, had orders to attack the wagons and ignore the warriors, and so they only fought when a fight was forced upon them.

But the Wanderpeople were also willing to fight hard, and when their arrows did not dissuade the men of Dannon-ska, they went in with swords. Fighting fiercely against forces superior in equipment, they managed to slow the enemy. And as the enemy were slowed, more wagons began to move.

Not that they were yet out of danger, for a wagon drawn by oxen does not move as fast as a horseman, even a horseman weighted down with heavy armour and weapons. Again and again the men of Dannon-ska attacked the hindmost wagons in the train, and again and again the warriors of the Wanderpeople sought to put themselves between the heavy cavalry and their prey.

It was a running fight all the way, worse even than the retreat when the Krondir had harassed them, for the men of Dannon-ska did not try to fight the warriors, but instead circled around and continually tried to strike for the wagons where no warriors stood in their way.

The wagons scattered, to some extent, and so did the warriors of the Wanderpeople. So also did the men of Dannon-ska, though they were little less dangerous for all of that. The Wanderpeople eventually ran out of arrows, and when they did so they could only try to come to close quarters and attack the heavy cavalry with swords. In such cases, the heavy cavalry often had the upper hand, though occasionally if enough of the Wanderpeople could come to the attack, they could overwhelm a smaller force of heavy cavalry.

It was a long night, a dreadful night, and only the eventual scattering of all the wagons of the Wanderpeople saved them. Finally, toward dawn, the heavy cavalry of Dannon-ska broke off the fight and rode on across the plain toward their city. They carried some captives with them, for all that the Wanderpeople could do to prevent them, and behind they left the Wanderpeople in ruins.

Fatha twice had had horses killed under him, and was now riding on a heavy cavalry horse which Jochon had somehow acquired. He had several nicks, scrapes, and cuts, none serious, but he could not worry about his wounds, remembering the wagons of his people burning along the way, the dead men, women, and children, who lined their track.

He presently had about forty warriors around him, not all by any means from the Clans which had asked for his protection. His protection! That was a bitter thought, for he had at the last been unable to protect any of them. How many had escaped, he wondered? In the morning, they would see to that. At the present, best gather whatever they could.

He looked around at the men with him. "Go out, gather whatever wagons you can find, and bring them here. We will see what we have remaining."He noticed that even men of the larger Clans agreed, even men whom the King of Kings had once had to threaten with death to make them accept Fatha's orders. And he noticed as well that Etiar of the Krondir was among the group, as well as three other Krondir.

"Have you seen anything of our wagon, Jochon? I know we got off early, but that would be no guarantee of safety this night."

Jochon shook his head. "Like you, Fatha, I have been busy. I could try to find them if you wish."

"Now? No, looking for a specific wagon at this time of night would be futile. We will see what happens in the morning."

More and more wagons and Krondir carts gathered as dawn lightened the sky. By now, Fatha knew his wagon was not one of those near him.

35. Aftermath of Disaster

"No one has seen your wagon, Fatha, but that means little. They may have scattered beyond the reach of our scouts. We will find them."

Fatha nodded, absently. Jochon's reassurances could not comfort him; he had seen sufficient of the horrible savagery wrought by the men of the city. Until he found the wagon, found Grannon and Narolen and Temo, he would not allow himself to hope.

Despite that, there were so many other calls on his time, so many decisions to be made. There were families which were practically destitute, with no wagons nor possessions beyond the clothing on their backs, often even no men left to herd whatever cattle might be left to them. What provision could be made for these people?

In the ordinary course of the life of the Wanderpeople, no person was without relatives among the Clan, and some or all of those relatives would come to the aid of families left destitute. But if the system of relationships broke down, where did the destitute turn? Fatha suggested and sometimes dictated arrangements where necessary, trying to see that everyone had somewhere to turn for necessities.

Some of the Krondir were among those left without possessions, and they needed help as well. Whenever possible, he assigned other Krondir to look after them, but he was, on occasion, forced to mix them with the Wanderpeople.

Midway through the morning, when the situation was fairly well in hand, Jochon brought a woman to Fatha. Smoke and tears and blood streaked her face. She had a freshly bandaged cut on her neck, and she was clearly weary. "Fatha," said Jochon quietly. "This woman has news you should hear."

The woman looked up at him, her eyes blank with exhaustion. "We saw your wagon burn, Fatha. The Iron Men rode in just ahead of us and attacked your wagon. We went around them, for there was nothing we could do. When your wagon was burning, they came after us. Warriors of the clans held them off for a time, but at last, they caught up with us. I was struck down early on," she touched the bandage at her neck, "and when I came to my senses again, they were gone, the wagon was burned, and my babies were dead. My babies---" she put her hands over her eyes and broke into weeping.

Jochon led her aside and gave her into the care of some women who tried to comfort her. Jochon came back to Fatha.

"Did you find out where it happened?"

"More or less."

"Lead me there." Fatha felt nothing at all. Inside himself, he knew that Narolen and Grannon were almost certainly dead, but he felt no emotion at all.

Jochon looked at him, then nodded. Shortly after that, they were on horseback, riding back along the trail of destruction in the company of ten warriors.

From time to time, they found wandering oxen who had somehow survived the destruction of the wagon they had hauled. Fatha heard himself say, as though it were a stranger speaking, "We had best have someone round up all those; they will be needed."

After they had been riding a while, Jochon said, "This is where the scouts found her. She said that she had been walking two hours or so, but you saw the state she was in. Her estimate of time would not be very reliable."

They rode on. They came to a small hill on which were the smouldering ruins of three wagons. Jochon surveyed them, then pointed to one. "This one, I think." Fatha looked too, but he could not see how this one was any more likely to be the woman's wagon than any of the others. There were dead bodies around them all, most of them children, to be sure, but what of that? Perhaps it was the fact that there were no dead women near this particular wagon.

It was possible to backtrack that group of wagons. They had been part of a major group of wagons and had left a very visible trail, marked by charred ruins here and there. Fatha wondered as they rode whether he could distinguish his own wagon, and realized even as that thought came to him he would recognize the corpses of his family, at any rate.

They came up another hill. There was a dead man who had, from the looks of things, been trapped under his horse when it had been killed. He had worked his way free and dragged himself a few yards further along in the direction of the flight of the Wanderpeople before death had finally claimed him. The charred wreckage of a wagon lay on the hill, and there was the body of a cavalryman of Dannon-ska nearby to show that the people of that wagon had not died easily.

But there was no sign of them. Had they escaped, or had they been killed elsewhere? Or had they been thrown inside the burning wagon? The cavalry had done that sort of thing before.

He glanced at the oxen, dead in their traces, then looked again. He recognized the off ox, and well he might, for that was the ox for which he had laboured at Hadar-esh! This was his wagon. "Jochon!"

But Jochon was already at his elbow. "Ah, Fatha! This is it, then!"

"Yes. But what of Naro and the babe?" He looked in the embers of the fire. He could see no sign of them there. "We will wait until the fire dies, so we can look into the embers. If they were cast inside, there will be some trace, however little."

Jochon made as if to say something, then thought better of it. He went back to the men and spoke to them. Fatha remained there, staring into the embers, occasionally imagining that he saw something. His horse, the heavy cavalry horse that Jochon had gotten for him, began to shy away from the fire and the dead oxen. Fatha reflected that a well-trained warhorse ought to have been made used to such things, but he got down and stood, holding the horse firmly by the reins.

Jochon was beside him. "Fatha?"

"Leave me alone, Jochon."

"Fatha, it is Temo. He is alive."

Fatha whirled. "Where? Does he know what happened to them?"

"He is over here." Jochon took the reins from Fatha's hand and tossed them to one of the other men, then led Fatha off to the man whom Fatha had thought to have died trying to crawl away. It was indeed Temo, though he had been badly hurt when the horse fell on him, and had afterward apparently been thrust in the chest by a cavalryman's lance. His eyes were open, and recognition flashed in them when Fatha knelt over him.

"Sorry, Fatha," he said. It came out in a couple of painful gasps. "Tried."

"I'm sure you did, Tiyo. Don't worry. We're here now."

The boy shook his head. "Fatha, they're not dead!"

"What?"

"Leader of cavalry. He recognized them. Told men take them along, captives, maybe hostages."

"You're sure?" Fatha gripped him by the shoulder.

"Sure." The boy's eyes closed. Fatha was on the point of shaking him to wake him when he caught himself. Temo was still breathing, but his condition was not good.

Fatha looked up. "Do what you can for his wounds, make him comfortable. Jochon, come with me."

36. Wrath of the Wanderpeople

They rode back to the main body of the Wanderpeople as rapidly as the state of their horses would allow. When they arrived, Fatha immediately sought out Duinifaire. The small man had been quite busy, for though many of the Wanderpeople were wary of him and many more frankly fearful, those who had serious wounds and injuries were able to overcome much of the fear.

Nor had he had an easy time of it in the retreat, for he had clearly suffered more than one wound himself. He had managed to come through, though, and Fatha wondered how much his magic had helped him.

"Ah, Duinifaire!"

Duinifaire looked up. "Ah, Fatha! It is that you still live, then?"

"Yes, and I see that you have survived as well. I need your help, Duinifaire."

"What sort of help?"

"This sort of help." He gestured at the wounded people about Duinifaire. "Temo is badly wounded, perhaps even dead by now. I need you to do what you can for him."

"Hm. If it is that he has already died, I can do nothing for him, you know."

"I know that. I do not need miracles, only that you do what is possible."

Duinifaire looked at his wagon and his oxen. "My animals are tired, but perhaps it is that we can manage a short journey. Will you ride with me?"

"Certainly. Jochon, keep the people together. You are in charge until I return." He turned his horse, but Duinifaire called him.

"Fatha!"

"Yes?"

"You have already ridden that horse hard. Come up on my wagon with me."

"Your wagon?"

"Yes. It is that I must take the wagon with me, you know, and you need not travel any faster than I do. Come."

Fatha hesitated, then handed the reins to Jochon. "Jochon, take care of my horse, will you?"

Jochon hesitated, then took the reins. "Bring him back safe, Duinifaire." he said, and his voice held no trace of jest.

Fatha got up into the wagon and sat on the seat beside the small man. Duinifaire urged his oxen into motion, and away they went. Fatha restrained his impatience, knowing that there was no way to hurry the oxen. Slowly they went down the hill where the Wanderpeople had gathered. Then slowly they went up the hill beyond, the oxen leaning into the traces.

As they neared the top of the hill, Fatha began to feel weary. The rocking of the wagon relaxed him, just as it had always done since the time when he was a child.

A Dark Presence stood on his left side, a threatening presence. But there was a Bright Presence on his right, and he sensed that the Bright Presence kept the Dark away.

A harsh voice spoke out of the Darkness. "You thought you could delude me so? He has it, I know."

"And if he does? Can you take it from him? You have failed so far."

Again, the voice of the Dark Presence. "You cannot protect him forever!"

"Perhaps not, but then I need not protect him forever, only for long enough to bring things to order. Then I can take it back, and it will be too late for you."

"Do not boast too early! I am not altogether helpless, you know."

There was a sudden jarring bump, and Fatha woke. "Hah! What was it you ran over there? Whatever it was, I thank you, for I had no wish to see the end of that dream."

"Dream? You dreamed?"

"Yes. It was a strange sort of dream, two beings, one Dark and one Light, in a confrontation over something I possessed. I am not sure that I understand it, but then it was only a dream. Or was it? Can you tell me anything about it, Duinifaire?"

"Perhaps I might, but as you see, it is that we are practically at our destination."

And when Fatha looked up, he saw they were indeed coming up the hill toward the place where Temo lay. He had not thought that so much time had passed, and when he saw the position of the sun, he suddenly remembered how Duinifaire had met them three days out of Endolashan to give them a warning that he had received that morning.

He thought of asking how they had come so far, so quickly, but even as the thought came to his mind, he realized Duinifaire would not be likely to be able to explain it to him. All he could do was be glad of it.

Temo was still living, unconscious, but holding on to life by one slim thread. Duinifaire looked at him, then shook his head.

"Is there nothing to be done for him?" Fatha asked.

Duinifaire started and looked around at Fatha. "Oh, I think I can save his life." He held up a warning hand. "That is no promise, mind you! It is that I will do what I am able, and perhaps save him. Now leave me to my work."

Fatha stood back, then, and watched as the small man went to work. Duinifaire surveyed what the warriors had already done for Temo's wounds, and most of it he left alone. He removed the bandages from the chest-wound, and sprinkled a little of some kind of powder in it, then replaced the bandages. He took a little flask, poured a few drops of potion into a cup, then held up the young man's head to pour the liquid into his mouth. Temo swallowed, and Duinifaire nodded.

That done, he sat back on his heels and watched.

Some time passed, and no one moved. After about an hour, a warrior came over to Fatha and asked, "What is he doing?"

Fatha, without taking his eyes off the two, shook his head. "I do not know, but he did say that he hoped to save Temo's life. I would as soon not interrupt him until he shows that he is ready for interruptions."

"We wait here, then?"

Now Fatha looked around. "No, not all of us. Leave three here, then take the rest and look around the nearest wagons, see if there is anything to be salvaged. Anything at all, weapons or cooking pots, whatever you can find."

The man hesitated, then went. Fatha paid no more attention to him.

***

There was a tall white tree growing up out of the ground, tall and straight, many-leaved, bearing blossoms of white. Around the trunk of this tree stood several men in armour, bearing swords in their hands. Outside this circle of guards danced several misshapen black beasts who carried axes in their hands. From time to time, the beasts would rush in, trying to get past the guards, to strike at the trunk of the tree. Though the guards were constantly vigilant, they were outnumbered, and occasionally an axe would strike the tree and gouge its trunk.

Fatha could see that much depended on the determination of the beasts; if they persisted, eventually they would destroy the tree, despite the efforts of the guards.

Then one beast looked toward Fatha, yellow-eyed, fangs showing in a grin of delight at destruction. Suddenly, the beast's expression changed to one of fear.

Fatha woke up with a start; the wagon was just rolling over the last hill before the camp of the Wanderpeople. It took him a moment more to remember what had happened; they had at last loaded Temo carefully into the wagon, then he and Duinifaire had set out again, leaving the other men to bring back what they had salvaged, including whatever live oxen or horses they could find.

Duinifaire was looking at him. "You dreamed again?"

"Yes, and it was a strange dream." He described the dream to the small man, who nodded.

"It is that my wagon often brings dreams. They may be dreams to tell what will happen, dreams to tell what has happened, or dreams to tell of things which will never happen."

"And which would this be?"

"Ah, now, it is that this is hard to say. The interpretation of dreams is not something at which I claim much skill."

"Can you guess?"

The small man's eyes lighted up briefly. "It is that any man can guess, and some guess better than others. But what will my guess do? Will it make you act differently? And if so, is it that I ought to risk causing you to act differently through some guess of my own?

"So let me say only this: It seems you have a great work to do, to defend the Tree."

"And what does the Tree represent?"

Duinifaire shrugged. "I suppose that you will find that out eventually. And now comes Jochon to be sure that I have brought you back safely."

And indeed, Jochon was galloping up the slope toward them, leading an extra horse. He paused by the wagon to look searchingly at Fatha, as though seeking some sign of hurt or injury.

"Yes, Jochon, I am back and I am safe."

Jochon smiled a tight little smile. "And Temo?"

"He sleeps in the back of the wagon. He will probably live."

Jochon swung the extra horse around next to the wagon seat, and Fatha swung himself up into the saddle. He then turned to look down at Duinifaire.

"Duinifaire, thank you. I already owe you much, now I owe you more."

Duinifaire shook his head. "Let us not talk of owing and being owed, Fatha. It is that I have done as you asked, and am glad to have been able to do so much."

For a moment, Fatha looked down on him, then nodded, turned and rode away with Jochon.

The Wanderpeople gathered around Fatha, looking up at him expectantly. Finally, one man spoke. "Fatha, what do we do now?"

The speaker was an older man, a Clanchief, though not one chief who had accepted the protection of Fatha's group. Fatha looked around. They were all expecting his leadership and advice. This was something new for the Wanderpeople! A man outcast from his own Clan, and several hundred others were looking to him for leadership. If it were not for the loss of Grannon and Narolen, he might feel triumphant.

But they were waiting for him to speak. "What do we do now?" Black anger was coming over him, but he held it back, making plans in his head even as he spoke. "Now, we have our revenge! Listen, for years we of the Great Mother Plain have endured the sneers, the condescension, the insults, even the injuries of the people of the cities. Was not this last night only more of the same? And is it not time, and more than time, that we should strike back, pull their kings down from their thrones, and show them that the folk of the Plains are not to be trifled with?"

He looked around again. There was delighted approval in many faces, doubt in others. He continued to speak. "'Ah, yes,' you say, 'But how is this small group to be revenged on the peoples of the cities? They are many, and they are behind high walls. We are few, and we have nothing to break down the walls.'

"But listen to me! Think, is there any man of the Wanderpeople who has never wished himself able to deal with the people of the cities as they deserve? They will join us! They must join us! We will go to the Clans and compel them to come with us. And if any thinks that such compulsion might be wrong, think of what has been done this last night! Is there any of you who has not suffered loss? Is there any of you with no reason to see the cities humbled?" He paused. "Is there any of you who will follow me?"

The answer was a roar of approval from hundreds of throats.

37. The Wanderpeople Gather

Fatha left his warriors on the hill overlooking the camp, and rode down alone, save for Jochon and a few others. They had done this often enough that they hardly needed orders.

Among the group that rode with him was Goma, whom Fatha had condemned to death so long ago. Goma had ridden and fought in the retreat's night from Endolashan, had performed amazing feats of courage and sometimes even blind stupidity, though for all of that he came out with only a few scratches on his arms and one gash across his cheek. Perhaps when this was over, Fatha thought, he ought to remit Goma's sentence. For now, though, there were more important matters to be dealt with.

The chief of the Clan, accompanied by a few men of his own, rode out to meet them.

They paused a little distance from each other and surveyed each other. Fatha could see the curiosity in the Clan-chief's eyes, for in this group were several outcasts, and several more with Clan-symbols still on their cheeks. And in addition there was Etiar, clearly not of the Wanderpeople, and probably known to the Clan as one of the dreaded Krondir.

But all this strangeness sufficed to make the chief very wary. "What do you want here?"

"We want your help."

"Help?" There was surprise on the chief's face now, for an outcast was speaking for this group. But there was also suspicion. "What sort of help?"

"It has been decided that the people of the cities should be humbled. We are gathering forces to do so."

"Indeed?"

"Indeed. Have you heard how the King of Kings of Endolashan hired Wanderpeople for his war against the Krondir? Have you also heard that when it came time to pay them, he instead sent the King of Dannon-ska to attack them by night, to slaughter them and destroy their wagons? We have decided that it is time for revenge."

The chief shrugged. "What is that to us?"

"We have come first to ask your aid in this venture."

The chief sneered. "And in this venture, an outcast speaks for all? Be off with you! We have no time for such foolishness!"

Fatha urged his horse forward and clubbed the chief out of the saddle with his fist.

Fatha then dropped to the ground beside the chief, drawing his sword as he did so. He lay the point of the sword at the chief's throat. "First, we come to ask aid, and if it is not given freely, we demand it." His voice was cold and hard. "Your first choice was to accept freely. Your second choice is to accept or to die, after which I will negotiate with your successor, or your successor's successor. But your people will join us."

He did not have to look up to know that his own men were gathered around him, and that the larger force on the hillside waited for only the word to come down. The chief looked up at him with pure hatred in his eyes. "So be it, then. If we have no choice, we have no choice."

"Good." Fatha stepped back and allowed the chief to come to his feet. "Have your wagons swing in at the rear of ours and join the march. Bring your own wagon up to the head of the line to march with the chiefs."

Fatha swung back up onto his horse. They rarely had to resort to violence, though he was always ready if it was necessary. In his mind was the thought of Narolen and Grannon in captivity, and with that thought in mind, he could not waste time trying to convince people with long arguments. If agreement was not immediate, then it must be forced. More often than not, even when the agreement was forced, after a time it became more wholehearted. After all, there would be a share in the plunder to be taken when the cities fell, would there not?

On they went, their numbers steadily increasing. And as their numbers increased, the easier it was to convince others to join them.

There came a morning when Fatha looked over his following and decided that they were very near to enough. Jochon was at his side, as ever, and seemed to read his thought. "A very different situation from the one we were in a few months back."

Fatha nodded. In the beginning, he had had to restrain his impatience; though attacking the cities was very important, there were things of more immediate importance. Though they were all willing to put whatever goods they had at the disposal of those who were left with nothing, the fact was that they had little to share. They still had the bulk of their cattle, and they convinced those who had received the gold which had been distributed to use it to provide for the rest who needed it.

"There was a time," Fatha agreed, "When it looked as though we were going to be spending the rest of our lives just ensuring that the few people with us had clothing and shelter. I think the village shops and artisans had never had such requirements put on them."

"And here we are---. Look!" Jochon was suddenly pointing at a plume of dust in the sky to the west of them.

"Ah, wagons! Get the men, let us go!"

And again, in a very short time, they were riding up to a large train of wagons. As they came nearer, a sense of familiarity suddenly struck Fatha. It was a moment before he realized that this was his Clan, the people who had cast him out.

For an instant, he was on the verge of running away, followed by a sudden desire to order a wholesale slaughter. Good sense took hold, however, and he continued boldly forward.

It surprised him not at all to find that Yopan, the shaman, was the Clan-chief. Yopan recognized Fatha almost immediately and was in a state of shock for a moment. His next reaction was to begin frantically shouting at his men to kill these people.

Fatha held up a hand. "Stop!"

Such was the authority in his voice that they stopped, at least long enough for him to speak. "All of you, listen! I have not come to wreak vengeance or any such thing, instead I have come for your help. And while you could easily kill me, notice the warriors behind us; if I die, they will quite certainly slaughter you to the last man, woman, child, and ox.

"But I have no intention of doing you harm. Will you listen?"

Yopan, however, broke out into a continued gabble of commands to his men to kill Fatha now, quickly. It was clear one or two of them were not completely in agreement with whatever arrangement had made him chief, for they looked at him contemptuously. Two others, however, drew their swords. Jochon and Goma moved in quickly, each taking one and flinging him to the ground.

Others, even those who had not at first obeyed Yopan's commands, reached for swords. Fatha shouted again. "Hold! Stop this, all of you! I have given my word that I mean you no harm! Now listen!"

Yopan calmed himself slightly, enough to sneer, "Word of an outcast! What is that worth?"

Fatha stared into his eyes. "How the Clan is fallen! By the teeth and toes of the Clan-spirit, the Clan that was once led by a man named Grannon is now led by a babbler barely fit to ride in Grannon's dust!

"I have no time to waste here! We have a task to do, and we will do it. You have the option of joining us or being our foes. And before you allow Yopan to answer for you too quickly, think about what being our foes will mean." He gestured behind him at the warriors, ready for battle.

"We will talk about this for a time," said one of the men with Yopan. They withdrew a little and spoke among themselves. It was clear that Yopan was against the matter, vociferously against, but there were others there with cooler heads.

One of them came forward. "If we agree to join Fatha, will you be seeking to come back and replace Yopan?"

"Replace Yopan? No, I have no intention of doing that. I have my own people, and I am their leader. You may have Yopan as your leader, and welcome to him."

The man rode back to his group. They discussed the matter a little more, then finally the same man came out again. "We will join you, Fatha, so long as you have no intention of recovering your place in the Clan."

"I do not."

The other looked at him, nodded, and rode back to the waiting group.

38. The Attack on Dannon-ska

They gathered around the city of Dannon-ska, waiting. The King had sent out a delegation to demand the usual tribute for passing through his territory. That delegation had been sent back with word that tribute was not forthcoming; rather, the Wanderpeople demanded that the city of Dannon-ska should open its gates and surrender itself.

The City, of course, had closed itself up and prepared for defence. They had been attacked by Plainsfolk before and had developed a method of dealing with such attacks. If the Plainsfolk were too many for their army to meet in the open, they would close up the gates and wait. Usually, after about a week, the army of Clans would break up and wander away. Eventually, even if the besieging army had not melted away completely, it would be small enough to be defeated by the army of Dannon-ska.

All the warriors in Fatha's army knew this, and they wondered about it. Fatha assured them he had taken this into account, and that his plan did not include sitting around and waiting, nor did it include assaulting the walls and the terrible casualties that would involve.

For the first day and night, they waited. Some chiefs came and asked Fatha, "Why do we wait? Why do we not attack immediately?"

"Because they expect us to attack immediately. I have a plan, and my plan involves confusing them first. They and their leaders know that a gathering such as this must make an attack almost immediately, otherwise Clans begin to lose interest.

"When we do not attack, they will begin to wonder. Are we incompetent, which means that they are safe? Or do we have some sort of plan in mind which has not occurred to them? When we do attack, therefore, the attack and the manner of it will take them by surprise."

Jochon watched the questioners ride away. "It will take them by surprise if Goma can carry out his part properly."

Fatha nodded. "True."

He maintained the tight control of himself which he had begun those months ago after the night of the attack. There was a part of him that wanted to lead his army in to attack the walls, to fight, to strike with the sword until the city was overwhelmed and Narolen and Grannon rescued. But he knew in his mind that such an attack would be futile, worse than futile, for not only would it be bound to fail, it would also destroy the army he had gathered. And he must not destroy that army, for it was likely that the attack on Dannon-ska would have to be followed by attacks on the other cities, if only to prevent the King of Kings from making war against the Wanderpeople.

Fatha looked up. Jochon was regarding him carefully. "Is something wrong?"

Jochon shook his head. "Nothing is wrong with me. I wonder about you, though."

"Me? Why?"

"You have changed, Fatha. It is like riding beside a statue carved of ice. You do not even get properly angry; you seem to have even calculated your rages, as though you have judged just when they are needed, and just exactly how much wrath will suit the particular purpose."

"Perhaps so."

Jochon waited for more answer, but Fatha said nothing.

Evening came, and the campfires of the Wanderpeople were lit. The evening meal was finished, and Fatha called young men to him who were to serve as messengers, and sent them off to take word to the commanders who were to lead the attack. "And tell them to remember to be careful when they get into the city; we have come to rescue the captives, and it would not do to kill by mistake the very people we came to rescue."

Again they waited. Silence settled over the army, save for the occasional stamping of horses' hooves and the odd murmur of conversation between men waiting and wishing that something would happen.

There was a sudden noise from the city. Heads came up. The sound came again, the sound of an alarm-horn of the Wanderpeople blowing. Fatha shouted something. He was not sure what, and the horsemen thundered toward the city. As they neared, they could see that the gates were open, and there was a fight going on between men trying to close them and men trying to hold them open.

The men holding the gates open had been sent in earlier, long before the army of the Wanderpeople had come close to Dannon-ska, with instructions as to what to do. They had entered as tradesmen and merchants, making their living and doing nothing out of the ordinary until this day.

Even so, it would be a hard fight; The gates were still blocked by struggling men, and if more soldiers came up, they might well prevent the Wanderpeople from penetrating far inside. Fatha and the people following him swerved off to ride around the city walls. As they went, they heard the sounds of battle beginning in earnest at the gates.

Fatha and his force rode round the wall, looking up at it. Suddenly Jochon pointed and shouted "There!"

Hanging from the wall was something pale, probably a piece of white cloth. Near it and around it were several rope ladders hanging down from the walls. "Up, quickly!" shouted Fatha. There were sounds of battle at the top of the wall where others of the group already in the city were holding off the soldiers until Fatha and his men could climb the ladders.

Fatha, holding his sword in one hand, went up one ladder as quickly as he could. As he neared the top, a face showed. Goma grinned in greeting.

There had been ten men with Goma in this group, and only five were still standing. But the alarm had only just been sounded, and the men of the city were barely realizing the danger. The first of the Wanderpeople to come up the ladders carried ropes, which they made fast inside the city walls, and tossed down to their comrades below. As the city men swarmed up in response to the alarm, there were a few moments during which the battle was in doubt.

But the Wanderpeople surged over the walls and down the stairs, then came back up the other stairs to take the men of the city from behind, causing greater confusion among them. The men of Dannon-ska did not lack for courage, and were fighting for their very homes, so there was a long time of swords gleaming and clashing in the moonlight, of bodies of men surging back and forward, before the Wanderpeople could clear a section of the wall and hold it fully.

And during all the time that they held that section of the wall, even when they were fighting for it desperately, more of their comrades were coming up and over, and going down into the city itself. Shortly after, a whole quarter of the city of Dannon-ska was full of bands of Wanderpeople rushing here and there, and they stretched too thin the warriors of the city to hold them.

The battle by now had gone beyond the state where any man could control it at all, save by sending in troops to this place or that attempting halt the enemy advance, or attempting to break through an enemy line. Here again, the Wanderpeople had an advantage, for there were too many streets and alleys for the city men to block. Each time the city men stopped the Plainsfolk in one place, they circled around the city men and moved on.

At last, a little toward dawn, Fatha and about a hundred others struck the rear of the troops holding the area around the gate. The men of Dannon-ska had by now heard that the Wanderpeople were over the walls behind them as well as facing them here at the gate. This fresh attack dismayed them too much to note how small the attack actually was. They began to break and flee. Before their officers could rally them, the situation was beyond retrieval. The Wanderpeople were once more pouring into the city through the gates.

But the end was not yet. There were still officers capable of rallying men, even a few, and so long as that still went on, the battle was not over. Now, however, the battle had a new focus. Most of the Wanderpeople had at least vaguely known of the layout of the city. This information had come by way of tales from traders and such like. Fatha, before the attack, had made a point of specifically finding and questioning traders, and making at least some of his men familiar with the way from the gate to the Palace.

It was toward the Palace that they now directed themselves.

The battle was now broken up into a thousand little skirmishes, here and there through the streets of the city. There was little direction to the fight, save that the Wanderpeople were making toward the Palace, and the warriors of Dannon-ska were fighting with them when they met.

It was the middle of the morning when Fatha, leading a small knot of mixed Wanderpeople and a few Krondir, found himself at the steps of the Palace. He was by no means the first, for around the courtyard and up the stairs were struggling knots of men, Wanderpeople and blue-cloaked Royal guards. The sight of the Palace gave him the strength to shake off his weariness. He charged across the courtyard, ignoring the soldiers of Dannon-ska, unaware even whether or not the men behind him were following.

Halfway up the stairs, a small band of soldiers met him. In the first moments of fighting, Jochon and the men behind had caught up to Fatha, and after a short but bitter fight, the soldiers were overwhelmed.

39. To Endolashan!

Fatha stalked through the marble halls of the Palace at the head of his men, like a grim wolf at the head of his pack. They finally came to the room where the King of Dannon-ska had fled at last, waiting on his throne for some miracle to save him.

His hair and beard, usually carefully oiled and curled, were now in wild disarray, and fear was in his eyes.

Fatha strode to the foot of the throne, grasped the King by the foot, and dragged him down. The King, in most circumstances a brave man, had just seen his city stormed and taken by enemies who ought not to have been capable of getting over his walls. He had seen his army practically wiped out, and now he faced a man with a scarred face and vengeance in his eyes.

"Where are they? Where are my wife and child?"

"They are not here!"

Fatha had known that there was only an infinitesimal chance that Narolen and Grannon would have survived the trip to Dannon-ska, but it surprised him at how much hope he had had.

"How did they die, then? Perhaps we could arrange a suitable death for you?" His voice sounded strange in his own ears.

"They are not dead! I swear, they are not dead! They have been sent to the King of Kings in Endolashan!"

Fatha drew a deep breath. "Indeed? For how long has the King of Dannon-ska been the servant of the King of Kings?"

"For some while, especially since the Krondir arrived. Endolashan is larger, has more resources to draw from, and the destruction wrought by the Krondir was more easily repaired there than here. Do you think that I really wished to do his work for him by attacking your camp at Endolashan? I had no choice! And when I sent word to him, I had your wife and son. He sent back a messenger demanding that they be delivered to him. And I had no choice there either."

"Indeed?" Fatha drew back his sword for a killing thrust, then changed his mind.

"I will spare you for the moment, and you shall come with me while we go to see if my wife and child are truly at Endolashan. And if you have been lying to me, I shall have to consider again what punishment is fitting. Do you change your answer? If they are truly dead, then speak now, and I will only kill you."

"No, no, I swear it, I sent them to Endolashan! You can question my servants!"

"And so I shall. In the meantime," he turned to the men behind him, "Bind him, keep him captive, and keep him whole. We shall need him later."

He looked around. "Jochon, have messengers sent to the commanders to bid them come to me this evening. We must make ready. I go now to rest; call me only if necessary."

But in fact, it was not Jochon nor any of the Clan-chiefs of the Wanderpeople who woke Fatha at last, but Duinifaire. When Fatha woke with a hand shaking his shoulder, he came up out of a dream which faded rapidly from his consciousness, leaving him only with a sense of something dreadful which had happened, or was about to happen.

He saw the large square face of Duinifaire above him and struggled to a sitting position. His limbs felt like lead, and his head felt as though someone had stuffed it with wool. "What is it?" he asked.

"It is that I need to have a word with you in private, and I chose this time, before your commanders come, and yet after you had had a little rest."

"That is very kind of you," said Fatha sardonically. "What may I do for you?"

"It is more a matter of what I may or may not be able to do for you. You may have noticed that those who seek to slay you for the sake of the amulet of Nik-Malo have done nothing for some time."

"'Yes, I had noticed that. I had hoped that perhaps they were growing weary of wasting their efforts."

Duinifaire shook his head. "I fear not. In fact, it is that I doubt they will ever grow weary. But that is not the difficulty. The difficulty is that I cannot seem to divine any sense of what they intend to do next."

Fatha said nothing.

Duinifaire went on. "Knowing our foe, knowing how they act, knowing what they have already done, it is that I was able to guess what they might do, and make preparations. Now, however, it is that I have no hints, only a few guesses. It is that I will not trouble you with those guesses; they could only distract your attention from more important matters.

"It is that I think, and let me assure you that it is only a thought, that you will have no further trouble until we have taken Endolashan. At that time, it is that I hope to have some better idea of what is happening."

"'Until we have taken Endolashan?' Is this a prediction?"

"Nothing magical about that." Duinifaire was smiling. "Even had you rescued Narolen and Grannon here, it is that it was the King of Kings who was at the bottom of it, and it was he on whom you most wished to be revenged. And it is that I know you well enough to know that by now you have a plan in mind for the taking of Endolashan as well."

Fatha shrugged. "Something of the sort, yes."

" It is that there is one thing more."

"Yes?"

“Not all the Wanderpeople are your willing followers. It is that there are many who would gladly see you dead, if it could be accomplished.”

“I had not forgotten that.”

“See that you do not.”

In the evening after supper, the Clan-chiefs gathered to hear Fatha speak of his plan for the taking of Endolashan.

He looked around at them, most waiting expectantly for his next pronouncement, several with impassive, unreadable faces, and he remembered Duinifaire’s warning.

“We go to Endolashan next. Yes, it is larger than Dannon-ska, but it is not invulnerable by any means. And we must get there quickly. Word will be coming to the King of Kings as to the fate of Dannon-ska, and he will try to take steps to see that the same thing does not happen to him. Within a week, he will have his men preventing Plainsfolk from entering the city.

“I have therefore already made certain arrangements; before word comes to him of the fate of Dannon-ska, I hope to have people already in the city.

“In addition, I plan to take the bulk of the army out tomorrow, carrying light rations, and riding straight across the Plain to arrive on the doorstep of the King of Kings before he has time to make ready. Are there questions?”

There were a few questions, and some protests from Clan-chiefs who did not feel that their people could march so soon. Fatha’s answer to that was to tell them they should gather as many as possible and be ready to march in the morning. There were a few other questions about the gathering of rations, most of which were dealt with quickly by Jochon. Then the chiefs drifted away to their own people.

A commotion outside his tent pulled Fatha up out of sleep. He came out, sword in hand, to investigate, and found Jochon standing over someone on the ground, hold his sword aimed at the throat of the supine figure. "What is it, Jochon?"

"I couldn't sleep, Fatha, so I took a walk around. And I found this, creeping toward your tent with a knife in his hand."

"Really? Who is it?" He stepped over and looked down. It was Yopan.

He felt no surprise; Yopan had hated him from long ago, and to be forced to follow Fatha would have been galling to him. Furthermore, being what he was, Yopan could never believe Fatha's assurances that he planned no revenge.

"Let him stand, but watch him." Fatha looked around to see who was nearby. "Ah, Tiyo. Gather a few others to help you and get round to as many of the Clan-chiefs as you can, and have them gather immediately. If they ask, tell them it is a case of attempted murder."

Yopan said nothing while they waited, nor did Fatha bother to question him. The shaman waited sullenly, with his head down, but Fatha did not fool himself into thinking that he would quietly confess all. He wondered what Yopan would say when the time came to speak.

In a fairly short time, the Clan-chiefs, as well as a number of others, had gathered around Fatha. Fatha debated for a moment sending the others away, declaring this a matter for the chiefs alone, but that was not the way of the Wanderpeople.

He saw in the crowd old Naucles, which brought a pang to his heart. He had taken the old man's daughter into exile with him, and now she was a prisoner and alone. Even though she might be cast out of the Clan, could a man simply cease to love his child, his youngest daughter? Naucles' eyes met his for an instant, and he knew he was right.

When he saw that most of the chiefs were present, he spoke. "This man was found stalking my tent with a knife in his hand. We have summoned you to hear judgement." He turned to the prisoner. "Yopan, what have you to say for yourself?"

Fatha's mind went back to that torch-lit night among the wagons when he, with his head filled with whatever drug had been used, had strived to answer that same question.

Yopan looked up and spoke defiantly. "This is a trick, a lie! I was summoned here, and when I arrived, this man," he thrust a finger towards Jochon, "attacked me! Then they held me here until you could arrive, so that they could kill me and pretend it was done according to law and custom!"

One of the other chiefs then asked, "Why should they do such a thing?"

"Because he was cast out of our Clan long ago, and now he seeks revenge on me, for I was a witness against him!"

Fatha would have spoken, but Jochon was too quick. "And if this were true, why summon everyone to hear the story? Do you not think it would have been simpler for me to have merely run you through with my sword, and afterwards tell the tale? Why would we risk letting you live to speak the kind of nonsense you speak now?"

There was muttering among the chiefs of the Wanderpeople now, ominous sounds and muttered calls for Yopan's death. But the shaman was not yet done. "Why not? Because you hoped with your lies to make this all seem according to custom. These are all your people. Will they believe you or me? And if they end in condemning me, will they not be concerned lest they themselves fall afoul of you in the future?"

Fatha spoke then. "Some of you have known me for a long time, some only for a matter of weeks. Who has known me to break my word? And did I not promise that Yopan should remain the head of his Clan? So now he accuses me of some involved trickery to remove him. Clan-chiefs, you know what my desire is, what is behind my gathering of the Clans together; to be revenged on the King of Kings, and to recover my wife and son. Would I waste my time to take some petty vengeance on this man?"

Yopan looked around and saw the condemnation on the faces of all the chiefs. He suddenly sprang forward to run, taking nearly everyone by surprise. Before he reached the ring of chiefs, Jochon had cut him down with one swift blow.

Fatha looked out at the assembly. "Let his Clan choose their own leader, with no interference from me. I am not of them. I have no part in their deliberations."

The people drifted away. Jochon found a couple of young men to bear the body of Yopan away. Fatha stood for a bit, then turned to go back into his tent.

"Fatha!"

He turned. Old Naucles was standing there, a little embarrassed. He was addressing someone who had been cast out of his Clan, someone who by rights ought not to be in his company at all. "Ah, Fatha."

"Ah, Naucles. What might I do for you?"

"Fatha, my daughter. Where is she?"

"You know as much as I do, Naucles. The King of Dannon-ska has claimed that she is in Endolashan."

"It is she, then? You only spoke of a wife and son, but you gave no names."

"And who else should it be, after you cast the both of us out together? Who else might I marry?"

"She was not cast out, Fatha! When we cast you out, she screamed and shouted at us that we were a pack of fools, being pushed by an evil woman and a man of no scruples. And when she saw that it could not be halted, she herself hitched the oxen to your wagon and, when we loaded you in it, she drove away. But she was not cast out!"

"But the Clan-symbol on her cheek was slashed away, just as mine---." He stopped, suddenly realizing the truth, realizing that Narolen had given up everything: family, friends, and all, for his sake!

"Naucles, I wish you had not told me this." He could barely force the words out. He turned away and stood for a moment. When he had recovered himself, he turned back.

"Naucles, we shall do all that is in our power to rescue your daughter and your grandson. And I doubt that you or anyone has more desire to see her safe than I. Go back to your wagons; your people will be needing your wisdom at this time."

Fatha went back to his bed, but he did not sleep again that night. In the morning, though, he was still the first on his horse. And when the force had gathered, he looked at them and said, "To Endolashan!"

"To Endolashan!" they answered and followed him as he rode.

40. The Assault on Endolashan

On the plain beyond the sight of the city of Endolashan, they met with a man of the Wanderpeople. He was short, somewhat squat, and browned by the sun to a shade just a little lighter than the leather he wore. "Ah, Fatha!"

Fatha recognized him as one of the scouts he'd sent forth, "Ah, Sendo! What word, then?"

Sendo shrugged. "It went well, Fatha. I have been watching, as you ordered, and either they have been slaying and secretly burying every Plainsman who enters the city, or our folk have been having no trouble. Just as you ordered, no more than a few at a time, most of them carrying hides or other things which could be traded in the markets. But this will differ from Dannon-ska, I fear."

"Oh yes, it will be different. The city is larger, for one thing, and we will have to attack at several different points. But I hope we will have the advantage of surprise."

Jochon spoke from his elbow. "Will we? What of the patrols we encountered? Even though we wiped them out, their absence will be noted."

"And perhaps the King of Kings will guess that they must have met with a superior force out on the Great Mother Plain, and perhaps he will even guess that this force will be coming against his city. But then what? He does not know that we are here, and our actual attack will still come as a surprise. Prepare the signal."

Shortly after, a Plainsman rode down toward the city of Endolashan, leading a spare horse. In one hand he carried a half-empty skin of beer, in the other he carried an alarm-horn. He stopped before the gate, a far bowshot away, and sounded his horn.

Slowly he rode around the walls, swaying in his saddle, alternately drinking from his skin of beer and sounding his horn. When the soldiers on the walls shouted down at him to ask what he was up to, he looked up drunkenly and called back to them something incoherent about the stars being too bright. Then he went on sounding his horn.

Eventually, one guard-captain decided that something should be done about him, and sent out ten heavy cavalry to either seize him or drive him away. Seeing the horsemen come out, the Plainsman rode rapidly away. As the cavalry pursued him, he seemed less and less drunk, going off rapidly to the north. The heavy cavalry never even came close to him; after a while, he shifted to his spare horse without stopping or even slowing much and was away again. The heavy-laden cavalry horses dropped far behind.

After dark, the army of the Wanderpeople moved once more. They would eventually come down on the city from three sides. Fatha was with those who would come in the main gate; others would come in the smaller gates on the north and the east, while still others would come over the wall as at Dannon-ska.

It was just barely possible that the King of Kings would have heard how the Wanderpeople had taken Dannon-ska, but the Wanderpeople had come straight across the Plain, at a pace which most fugitives, even mounted, could not match. It was unlikely that he knew anything about what had happened.

In the darkness, they could come up to within an easy bowshot of the walls without being seen, and this they did. Then they waited.

After they had been sitting thus for some time, Jochon stirred. "Teeth and toes of the Clan-spirit, I hate this waiting!" he muttered. "Give me a battle any day instead, whatever the odds."

"Nor do I like it," answered Fatha. "But even you must admit that we could not get through those gates or over those walls without help from within."

"You mistake me, Fatha. I do not have any better ideas as to how to get into the city. But that does not make the waiting any easier."

Fatha smiled slightly. "No, I suppose not."

Finally, even Fatha was beginning to fear that something had gone wrong, that one of the sections of the army had lost its way and had not gotten into position. He was just wondering if he ought to launch the attack without further delay when he heard a thin, far-off shriek. He saw Jochon's head come up. There was another thin shriek from far away, then a nearer one, from the north side of the city. Jochon looked at Fatha, who nodded. Jochon raised his bow and launched an arrow up toward the city. As it left the bow, the wind passing through the perforated head caused it to whistle shrilly.

They waited again. There was a commotion from the gates, the sound of the great doors being rolled back, the sound of battle within. Suddenly, they could see a torch in the gateway, waving back and forth vigorously.

"There!" Relief was evident in Jochon's voice.

"Forward!" shouted Fatha, and the Wanderpeople rode for the gates.

By the time they reached the gates, they were going at a gallop, and they barely slowed as they crashed through the struggling men.

41. Almost Rescued

Unlike at Dannon-ska, where the garrison had been on the alert and ready to turn out at a moment's notice, the city of Endolashan was almost totally unprepared. There were indeed soldiers in the guardhouses by the gates, there were soldiers ready to rush to the walls, but they had had no inkling that an enemy was coming, and the total garrison was by no means was at arms.

But this did not mean that the battle was instantly over. Most of the men of the garrison were experienced fighters. Many had seen fighting in the war against the Krondir, and despite the surprise and confusion, most of them fought where and when they could.

Fatha remembered very little of the fight as individual incidents, only that there were men before him and he was fighting them.

Suddenly it was dawn, and he and several hundred others were at the foot of the Palace steps, facing the Bodyguard of the King of Kings. All this was reminiscent of the battle of Dannon-ska, save that the Palace was larger, and the Bodyguard, besides being more numerous, were dressed in black and silver.

More of the Wanderpeople were coming up now. Fatha drew a deep breath; it was going to be hard fighting, for the Bodyguard were fresh, something which could not be said for his own troops. He looked around. Jochon, still at his side, grinned at him.

"Well? Do we stand here until noon?"

Fatha smiled back. "No, I suppose not." He looked around at the men who were looking at him, waiting for a signal. "In there," he pointed at the Palace, "is the Great One, the King of Kings, the one who betrayed us and tried to destroy us after we had served him faithfully! Let us go find him, drag him from whatever chair he hides under, and ask for an accounting!"

He started forward, and the Wanderpeople came with him. A few had bows and arrows with them, and arrows zipped over the heads of the Wanderpeople into the ranks of the Bodyguard where they stood on the stair.

The Bodyguard fought bravely and well, but there were simply not enough of them. The arrows helped, for taken straight on, the bows of the Wanderpeople could drive an arrow through the scale armour the Bodyguards wore, and even when the front ranks were at close quarters, there was room to send arrows up into the rear ranks. And that, in turn, meant that there were fewer behind to step into the gaps torn in the front ranks.

Holes appeared, and Wanderpeople flung themselves into these holes. The holes turned into gaps in the line, and the line turned into knots of men clad in black and silver struggling against men in brown leather. Fatha suddenly found the stairway clear in front of him and charged upward.

He did not look back to see if anyone followed him. The doors of the Palace were shut and barred, but the Palace had never been intended as a fortress. He heaved his shoulder against the door and it gave hardly at all. More of his warriors were up around him now, and he looked around. There was a small stone bench to the right of the door.

"Here, some of you take that bench and have this door down!"

It took a moment, because almost everyone wanted to handle the bench and there was room for only two on a side, but eventually it was being swung in a rhythm against the door, which shuddered and shook.

Once, twice, they hit the door. Three times and it began to crack. The fourth time, the bar gave way and the doors began to collapse inward. A fifth blow completed the job, and the Wanderpeople were swarming into the Palace even while the remnants of the Bodyguard of the King of Kings was still fighting on the steps.

But the battle was not over. As they rushed through the hallways of the Palace, they came upon other companies of the Bodyguard, who fought until they were overwhelmed.

In the throne room they came upon a confusion of Bodyguards and officers and unarmed officials, with the King of Kings there among them in armour, with a sword in his hand. The confusion made it impossible for the Bodyguard to close ranks around the King of Kings, though some of them did indeed try to stop the Wanderpeople. Some officers also attempted to intervene, and Fatha saw Vrast stand forward with a sword in hand.

He almost wished he could shout at his men to take Vrast alive, but there was half a room of screaming, rushing people between them. He turned his attention to the King of Kings.

He hardly bothered to fight anyone who came between them, mostly pushing them to one side to be dealt with by one of the many others who were with him. Then he was before the King of Kings. He brandished his bloody sword and shouted, "Come, King of Kings, Betrayer of Allies, Stench of the World, measure swords with me! Or perhaps, as at the Battle of the Knoll, you would prefer to be someplace else?"

The King of Kings brought up his sword and warded off Fatha's first stroke. Fatha easily parried his answering blow and spoke again.

"Tell me, did your predecessor actually die under Krondir arrows? Or did you make sure of him before you rushed back to make yourself King?"

The tall man pressed his lips together and said nothing.

"What now, O Great One? What will you do now that doom has sought you out, even where you thought to be safe? Where will you go? Where will you flee to now?"

The King of Kings was pale and sweating. In the first battle against the Krondir, he had run away, though no one dared say so to his face. In the second battle, he had arranged matters so that he himself did not come into battle until the end, when the Krondir were worn out. For all the might of the Empire over which he ruled, he was not himself a particularly brave man. And this night, in his own city, in his own Palace, he was faced with men he knew he had betrayed, men he knew to have every reason to kill him.

His blows went wilder, his parries became less skillful. He backed away from Fatha, flailing with his sword. Suddenly, Fatha, with a quick twist of his own sword, flipped the sword out of his opponent's hand. Even before the blade clanged to the marble floor, Fatha had his sword-point up against the throat of his foe.

"Well, Mardrast, no longer King of Kings? What have you to say now?"

Mardrast clenched his teeth and closed his eyes, waiting for the killing stroke. It did not come.

"Open your eyes, Mardrast. Open them! I shall not slay you just yet."

Mardrast opened his eyes.

"I came here seeking my wife and child, Mardrast. Where are they? Well, I hope?"

Mardrast's mouth worked for a moment, but no sound came out. Finally, he was able to rasp out. "Yes, they are well. I knew you would come if you lived, and I intended to use them as hostages to prevent your attack."

Fatha nodded. "I expected as much. That was why I had to be sure that our approach was secret and our attack sudden, so that you would have no chance to use your hostages. You will please lead me to them."

He knew suddenly that the fighting in the room had ceased. The Bodyguard had fought to the last, but several of the officers had cast aside their swords and surrendered. The unarmed officials were huddling in a corner, viewing the Wanderpeople with fearful eyes.

Fatha looked around. "Ah, Jochon! Pick a few men to come with us. Temo, take charge here. See that the prisoners are made secure. Hurt no one unless they resist you."

Mardrast led them along the hallway, a rope around his neck to prevent him from making any sudden dash for freedom. Not that it seemed likely; his shoulders slumped, and he walked almost as one who walks in a dream. He led them to a doorway where the marble floors and walls gave way to more common stone, and where the air had a stench to it of bodies long unwashed, and other worse odours.

This corridor had a row of thick wooden doors, each with a small window covered by a grill of metal bars. Mardrast continued down this corridor, glancing at each door as he passed. He finally stopped at the tenth door and waved a hand at it. "Here," was all he said.

"The key?" asked Fatha.

"My chamberlain has it. I have not seen him this night; doubtless he lies dead somewhere in the streets."

Fatha stepped forward, intending to call Narolen through the bars, but stopped. He had waited this long, he would wait a little longer. He looked at his men. "Two of you go find something to take this door down. The rest of us will wait here."

The two were back very shortly with an axe. This time, Fatha went to the door. "Naro," he called.

There was stirring inside. He spoke again. "Naro, it is Fatha. We have come to get you out."

Suddenly, her face was on the other side of the bars. "Fiyo! It is you! How did you come here? And Jochon!"

"A long story, Naro. Stand back from the door; we are going to have to cut it down."

The man with the axe stepped forward then and chopped at the door. Chips flew. The door was thick, made of very hard wood, and cutting through it was no easy matter. The one man found himself wearying long before the job was done and had to pass the axe along to another. In between times, they heard the sound of the baby crying within, frightened by the noise.

While they were still cutting at the door, Duinifaire came down the hallway. He had his double-headed axe in his hand, and it was clear from the look of him he had taken some part in the battle. Fatha remembered he had left Duinifaire behind at Dannon-ska, but he was not at all surprised to see the little man here.

"Ah, Duinifaire! Just in time, I see!"

"Ah, Fatha! Yes, just in time."

"What is it, Duinifaire? You bring a new warning?"

"Yes, after a fashion. It is that I have been working at it for some time, and all my powers and sources tell me that the next attack will come when you are reunited with your family. What it will be, I cannot say. It is that I thought it better to be here with you to do what I could when the time actually comes."

"Thank you." But Fatha's mind was only half on the warning being given by the little man, for at that time the door broke inward.

The gathered men of the Wanderpeople shouted encouragement; two more blows landed, then half of the door fell away, the other half still swinging on the hinges. Fatha stepped through to see Narolen, who was trying to comfort Grannon, look up and step forward as well.

A pillar of nacreous light descended on woman and child. Fatha leaped forward, arms outstretched, but the light disappeared, taking Narolen and Grannon with it.

42. Again to the Rescue

Fatha turned toward the door. Duinifaire was standing there, and for a single mad moment, Fatha's mind told him that all this was the fault of the little man. He almost reached for his sword, but then reason convinced him that if there were any hope of recovering his wife and son, he would need help from Duinifaire.

He walked out of the cell. "Jochon, see that he," Fatha thrust his chin toward Mardrast, "is put somewhere where he can be kept from harm and from rescue. Then have the commanders begin to organize their men. If that can be done, no doubt most of them will be busy with looting. Duinifaire, let us find a quiet place to talk."

Fatha paced the room, while Duinifaire looked up, an expression of concern on his face.

"It is that you may blame me if you wish, Fatha. It is something I ought to have seen."

Fatha shook his head. "No time for blaming, Duinifaire. What puzzles me is that they did not simply take me. I am the one who has the jewel."

"Oh, it is that they could not. Among its other powers, the jewel prevents just that. It is that it must be given away, and cannot be taken from you while you live, nor can it be taken by magic."

"And what happens now?"

"Any time soon, it is that someone or something will come to you with the offer to trade your wife and son for the jewel."

"And you hope to dissuade me?"

Duinifaire shrugged. "It is that anything I say will seem as though I am pleading my own case, and you might well think that I am merely hoping to dissuade you. And yet it is that I recall that when the King of Dannon-ska took your family away, you did not send to him to see what sort of bargain you might make for their safe return."

"When the King of Dannon-ska took my family, it seemed to me that there was a possibility of recovering them by force of arms. Where should I lead my armies now, and against what? I cannot ask this of them, even if they were willing to go."

Duinifaire shook his head. "No, that was not what I was thinking of. It is that an entire army would be more of a hindrance than a help. One or two might well make their way through, practically unnoticed, and perform the rescue before the guards were aware that a rescue was being attempted."

Fatha was standing still, looking down at Duinifaire. "Indeed?"

"Indeed. It is that it is a dangerous journey, and there will be battle, but boldness may well see us through."

"Hah! Then let us go now!"

The little man held up a hand. "One moment. Ought you not first to tell your men what is afoot? Think how they will feel if you merely disappear."

Fatha checked himself. "You are right, of course." He went to the door of the room and opened it. Jochon was standing there, waiting. "Jochon! Gather who you can of the Clan-chiefs in the throne-room, as soon as may be!"

Jochon looked up at him, a little surprised, then nodded and went off. Fatha went to the throne room to wait, and Duinifaire followed.

In the throne room, Fatha found that the prisoners who had been taken in the throne-room were still waiting there. Among them, he saw Vrast, a bloody bandage around his head. Fatha went over.

"Ah, Vrast!"

The warrior looked up. "Ah, Fatha!" He smiled, a little grimly. "I heard what he intended to do to you, and I hope you will believe that I protested. In fact, I protested so much that he banished me from his presence for three weeks." He paused.

"I feared that if they did not kill you, you would find a way to strike back. Our late King of Kings, however, is very capable of convincing himself that the truth is what he thinks it to be. He has learned better now, I take it?”

“Perhaps so. You will forgive me, I hope, but there are many matters to be taken care of.” He turned to the guards.

“This man has been my friend. Treat him well. See that all the prisoners are fed after you yourselves have eaten.”

He saw Goma nearby and walked over to him. “Ah, Goma!”

The young man turned and looked at him. “Ah, Fatha!” His eyes were still shining. “All this, and the sentence is still not carried out.”

“But very nearly so.” Fatha looked at the bandage across his chest.

Goma looked down. “This? Foolishness, this. One of our own men, in one of those cursed allies, swinging at everything around him. I would not be surprised to hear that he had his eyes shut the whole time.”

“Be that as it may, come with me.” He led the young man to the steps of the throne and called the people to attention. “You of the Wanderpeople, listen to me! Some of you, many of you, will know that this man, Goma, was condemned to death, the execution to be carried out by his placing his body in the way of enemies of the band. He has done so numerous times in the last year, and many of you can bear witness to it.

“And since he has served us so well and nobly, always taking the post of danger, never flinching, I therefore declare the sentence of death to be revoked. You will pass this word to all your fellows, that all the Wanderpeople may know."

There was a buzz of talk from the people around, and Fatha turned to Goma and gripped his hand.

"Fatha, you need not---!"

"Goma, I think the Wanderpeople would benefit more by your life than your death. And as I have said, several times you have placed your body between the band and its enemies. Always you have survived, and this tells me that perhaps you were not fated to die thus. You are free."

"Fatha, I---" Words failed the young man. Fatha clapped him on the shoulder.

"Go on, Goma. Find a place to rest. You have done enough, more than enough."

After the young man had gone, Fatha looked around. A majority, but by no means all, of the Clan-chiefs were present. Jochon was at his elbow again. Fatha called for attention.

He simply announced that he would have to leave them for a while, and that during his absence, Jochon would be in charge.

"No!" Jochon spoke quietly but vehemently. "Where you go, I will go also, Fatha. Do not think to leave me behind while you go off into some strange world of magical dangers."

"How do you know where I plan to go?"

"Was not Narolen snatched away by a pillar of strange light, such as the light that brought some of those magical Warriors? And where else would you be going but after her? I go as well!"

"But the danger---"

“Toes and teeth of the Clan-spirit! Do you think I care for the danger? You go to rescue Narolen, and I go as well. That is all that is to be said!”

Fatha looked down at Duinifaire, who shrugged and smiled. “One more brave man will not be a hardship.”

“So then.” Fatha looked out over the crowd and saw Chogu looking back at him. “Chogu,” he called. “Will you take this burden for me?”

“I will.”

“Good. Lead them as you see fit. If we are too long gone, then use your judgement as to when you go back out on the Plain.”

Chogu nodded. Fatha looked at Jochon, then at Duinifaire. “Shall we be going, then?”

About noon of that day, they rode out onto the plain, beyond sight of the city. This was at the suggestion of Duinifaire, who thought it better not to make them all magically disappear in the sight of the rest of the Wanderpeople. There was a pony found which Duinifaire could ride. They had gotten bows and gathered arrows. They had packed up food to feed them on the way.

Duinifaire could not hazard a guess as to how long it might take. “It is that it depends entirely on the wards and guards about the place we must go to. It is that I hope it can be done in less than a day, but time passes strangely in the land to which we will be going.”

“What can we expect there?”

“Expect? It is that we can expect what might not be expected. It is that there will be things of magic, and these I will deal with myself, in the main. It is also that there will be attacks by sword, spear, lance, fang, or claw; these I will mostly leave to you.

"And just as it was that you came to Endolashan quickly and by surprise, before Mardrast had time to make threats to you regarding Narolen and Grannon, so also we must do this by surprise. It is that it may be a matter of moments, moving quickly before he can find us and speak threats. And whatever command I give, obey it without argument, no matter how strange or perhaps even foolhardy it seems. You understand?"

"I think so," answered Jochon. Fatha merely nodded.

Once they were out of sight of the city, Duinifaire got down. "It is that I will produce the gate. It is that it will not last long, for its presence will shout out to our foe that we are there, and what we must do is to close it immediately so that he has no time to discover exactly where it is. Be prepared to move quickly."

He sat down cross-legged on the ground and stared into space. It seemed that he sat and stared for a long time, then suddenly there was a shivery shimmer in the air before him. It thickened and grew a little. Then he was up and going for the pony. "Now! Ride, quickly!"

They kicked heels into the sides of their horses and galloped into the shimmer in the air.

43. Beyond the Gate

The horses stumbled as they came through, the ground here being about half a hand-breadth lower than the ground from which they had come. They danced around for a moment or two, catching their balance, then the riders had leisure to look about them.

It was a strange world, for the hills were covered with an unnaturally pale grass; set here and there on the landscape were trees formed of crystal. The crystals were subtle shades of brown and green, but crystal nevertheless. The riders were on a path, and the path seemed to be formed of small round shiny pebbles, crystals again.

Ahead of them, along the path, stood a large castle. It too seemed to be made of crystal, clear crystal which glittered in the sun's light.

Fatha looked down at Duinifaire. "What now?"

"Along the path, toward the castle. Quickly."

They rode rapidly for a few moments, then Duinifaire shouted, "Left! Into the trees!"

They went into the trees, then paused. The little man looked up at the two. "It is that I have tried to make matters a little more difficult for him; it is that I have opened several doors around his country, all opening and closing at the same time. It is that he will first be concerned about many attacks; unless he looks in the one correct place, he will find nothing, which will make him wonder whether he is really under attack.

"It is that he will probably not find us quickly; if it is that we are unlucky, he might find us sooner than we wish. If that is so, it is that I shall have to take other measures.

"Now, along this path."

Fatha looked down and saw a path which had not been there before. It was smaller, narrower than the main one, and it wound among the crystal bushes.

"Have your bows ready," Duinifaire said. "It is that we may have avoided his gaze, but there are other things of danger here."

They rode quickly but warily. For a long while, there was no sound in the forest of crystal trees. Eventually, though, they heard small noises around them; shrill bird songs, small feet rushing among the bushes.

The noises increased. Suddenly there were snarls from the glassy thickets, and they were attacked. The animals which flung themselves out of the brush looked like wolves, wolves with glittering black fur and sharp teeth.

The men had been expecting trouble for some time, so when the first attack came, the two bows sung in unison, and one wolf went down. After that, the wolves were too close for bows; the men drew their swords.

Fatha cut down at one in a backhand stroke. The shiny black fur shattered into tiny shimmering black chips along the line of the stroke. He had little time to muse on that, for another was coming up on the other side. He struck again.

The battle was short but vicious. When it was over, four of the wolves were down and dead, while each of the horses had suffered at least one gash. None of the wounds was very serious, nor had they time to spend on bandaging; Duinifaire shouted, "Quickly, away!" and led them at a brisk trot.

Very shortly, they were coming near to the walls of the castle. All the brush had been cut down, baring the ground for the distance of about two bowshots from the castle walls. They reached the edge of that zone, then paused. "Now," said Duinifaire, but he got no further.

A great dark shape rose up, looking very much like a large rectangular blanket nearly twice the height of a man and nearly as broad. It was glossy and black and appeared to be made of small thumb-sized pebbles joined together. Though it seemed to have no eyes, it turned to them, and though it had no feet, it moved toward them, rippling and undulating.

Both Fatha and Jochon reacted automatically, raising, drawing, and loosing their bows in a a single movement. The arrows ripped through the thing, flying off to be lost in the crystal brush. It felt them, though, and hesitated before it came on, undulating gently, catching the light on its glossy surface.

Fatha watched it come, watched the light flickering off its surface, wondering at the beauty of it. Suddenly his horse jumped under him, and as he got the animal under control again, he saw the Duinifaire held a small dagger in his hand. He had apparently just pricked Fatha's horse with it.

"Don't stare at it," he shouted. "It is that it will trap you thus!"

Fatha now noticed that Jochon had shot two more arrows into the thing. He raised his own bow and began to shoot as well.

But the thing moved deceptively quickly, and suddenly it was looming over Fatha again. He kicked his horse into movement, slashing quickly at it with his sword as he went. It turned to follow him. Jochon rode in rapidly to strike at it from behind. It seemed to form an arm out of its own substance, and lashed out, striking the horse. The animal fell with a shriek. Jochon rolled free, stood, then dodged again as the beast turned on him.

Now it was Fatha's turn to ride in and distract the great black thing. Like Jochon, he struck at it with his sword, and as it had done to Jochon, it formed an arm, reached out, and struck.

But Fatha had seen that and was not taken unawares. He chopped at the arm, cutting away a bit of the crystalline stuff, which fell to the ground and lay there writhing.

Duinifaire had not been idle during this time, either. He had gotten down from his pony, being unused to fighting mounted, and was moving lightly on foot, stepping in and striking with his axe whenever there was an opportunity. And every time the axe struck it, the great beast shuddered and moved away.

It was dreadfully hard to kill; they cut and chopped at it, leaping back to avoid the arms it threw out at them, then moving back in to hew again. One such limb struck Fatha, the merest touch on the right arm, and he felt a bitter, searing cold, a cold which partially numbed his whole arm.

He switched his sword to his left hand, dodging another blow from the huge beast, and struck again, at the same time working the fingers of his right hand to try to recover the feeling.

Fearsome as it was, the beast could not watch in all directions at once, and whenever it moved on one of them, one or both of the others would attack from behind. And though it could strike out at those behind, it did so blindly, and usually missed. It also became clear that it could not strike out with more than one arm at a time, and as they discovered this limitation, they took advantage of it repeatedly.

Then Fatha noticed that with each arm chopped off, it grew noticeably smaller. Panting with exertion, he pointed this out to the others, and they worked at chopping off arms as they appeared. Eventually, the thing was no larger than a man, and its arms were shorter. It also moved slower now, as though it, too, was growing weary.

Finally, it broke off the struggle, rushing off into the brush. Duinifaire spoke. "Let it go! It is that we have delayed too long already. Gather with me, quickly!"

As they stood by him, he said, "It is that we still have some hope of getting into the castle unseen. It is that we cannot go by the main gate, of course, but we can probably go in by one of the lesser gates. It is that I will keep us cloaked as we move, and unless I am very clumsy, it is that I will get us through the door without being noticed. After that, I do not know."

Jochon's horse was dead and Fatha had dismounted during the fight, it proving difficult to fight that kind of in-and-out fight while mounted. They went in on foot, walking as quickly as they could.

They approached a small gate, a single heavy wooden door, and stood for a moment while Duinifaire moved his hands over the lock. Then he swung it open and motioned the two men inside. He came in after them and closed the door behind them.

"It is that this will not remain unnoticed for very long. Follow me!"

"You know where to go?" asked Fatha as they hurried after him.

"So should we all hope!" answered the little man, not looking back.

It was quite light within the castle, for the walls were translucent, allowing the sun's rays to diffuse as they came through; there was no glare, but light enough to see by. They hurried through hallways and up stairways, now taking a passage to the left, now to the right, in response to some clues which were not at all apparent to Fatha.

Suddenly they came round a corner directly into a party of eight black-furred Wolf-

Warriors of the sort that had been sent to attack Fatha once before. The three did not pause nor hesitate; they began the fight at once, striking before the Wolf-Warriors could draw their curved scimitars.

Even the element of surprise did not get them through the fight unscathed. When it ended, Fatha had a cut on his left arm, Jochon was limping on his right leg, and Duinifaire had taken a stroke to the chest.

Fatha would have paused to see how bad the little man's wound was, but he was given no time. "Come on, now! It is that we are discovered, and we have no time to waste!"

They were rushing through the corridors faster than before, for all their wounds and weariness. Finally, Duinifaire led them to a chamber in the upper levels. He touched a hand to the lock, gave a small hiss of dismay, then, with an expression of resignation, threw the door open.

It was rather a bare room, the only furnishings consisting of a heavy wooden table and a bed in the far corner. On the bed sat Narolen, holding Grannon close to her chest, while in front of the table, facing the door, stood a man.

After all they had come through, he seemed a very ordinary man, tall, dark-haired, wearing a coat of armour fashioned from small links of metal joined together. In one hand, he bore a long sword, unsheathed, and on his head was a rather plain metal helmet.

His eyes, however, were the yellowish eyes of a wolf, and his grin as he saw the three was more of a snarl.

"So you have come, have you? Hoping for a rescue? Three fools, come on an errand of fools! And I win!"

He gestured with his free hand; there was a crackling in the air around them, but nothing else. He looked a little surprised, but gestured again. Again, other than the crackling in the surrounding air, there was no result.

He frowned, then sheathed his sword. At the same moment, Fatha, realizing that this was his chance, perhaps his only chance, stepped forward, raising his own sword.

The man smiled, then gestured with both hands. Fatha stopped, and though he strained his muscles, he could not move. The man smiled again, then began gesturing again, with both hands.

Suddenly a cloud of light formed behind him, then faded; when it faded, nine men and women stood there. They were clad in robes of white, all save one wearing a jewel on a chain round the neck, holding a small child. When Fatha looked closer at that one, he saw it was Nik-Malo with Grannon in her arms.

But neither she nor any of the others seemed to pay any attention to Fatha or his companions. Instead, they were looking at the man in armour, who whirled to confront them. Fatha felt the power that bound his limbs drop away and was about to continue forward when Duinifaire grasped his arm.

"No! It is that you should leave this to them! Take your wife and son, and let us be leaving now, while we are still able!"

Fatha instantly saw the sense of that and rushed round the room to where Narolen was.

Narolen, startled and confused by what was happening; Fatha took her by her free hand. "Come, Naro, quickly!"

The scars on her cheek reminded him of his talk with Naucles. She had done that in order to accompany him into exile and had suffered for it. What could he ever do in return?

He saw her start to say something, then closed her mouth again, nodded, and came along.

The nine in white were still facing the man in armour as they left. None of them made any movement, but Fatha was sure that they were battling as hard in their own way as the Wanderpeople and Duinifaire had battled against the creatures of this strange land.

They were barely in the hallway outside the door when there was a strange tearing sound, and a long crack appeared in the crystal roof over their heads. Again they hurried down the hallways, downstairs, following Duinifaire.

Now and again there was the same tearing sound, and cracks would appear in the crystal, long cracks which appeared to run throughout the castle. Still, they went on. Narolen could keep up the pace even with Grannon in her arms, but Jochon was flagging. Fatha dropped back to help.

A jagged chunk fell from the crystal roof, bouncing and skittering along the glassy floor. "Go on, Fiyo, leave me be!"

Fatha only shook his head. He took Jochon's arm and threw it over his shoulders, and hastened on to try to catch up with the others.

There were other people in the hallways now, Wolf-warriors and strangely shaped servants. They paid scant attention to the fugitives, though, for they were also fleeing the castle, looking up in fear as cracks appeared in the building's fabric, dodging falling pieces of crystal, and running on.

44. Escape

As they finally came to the hallway leading to the door, they could hear a grinding and clashing back inside. The walls were less translucent from being so cracked and pitted; in the dimness the fugitives struggled to stay upright and to hold their places in the crowd that surged toward the exit.

At the door itself, things were even worse, for there was pushing and fighting to get outside. Duinifaire went in front, with Narolen immediately behind, carrying Grannon. On each side of her went Fatha and Jochon, fending off those who would try to push in. Several times it came to sword-strokes with the Wolf-warriors, but they finally reached the door and passed through.

They made their way to the edge of the crowd, and Duinifaire looked around. "It is that the Warriors will be attacking us again in a moment. Hold them off long enough for me to set up the doorway to home."

Indeed, he had barely gotten started when the first of the Warriors came at them. He was all alone, but he did not hesitate, leaping forward with his scimitar raised. Jochon cut him down before his stroke could land.

But that was only the beginning. Others of the Warriors had now noticed the strangers among them, and began to advance.

The Wanderpeople might not have survived had not a distraction taken place at that moment. With a terrible grinding, shrieking crash, the castle began to fall in. Possibly the only one not to pay any attention to it was Duinifaire, who was deeply engrossed in his own work.

But when the last bit of crystal had collapsed to the ground leaving a pile of glittering shards, the Warriors began to howl and spring forward. Then, amid the shouting and clashing of swords came Duinifaire's call: "Fatha, Jochon, Narolen come quickly!"

There was no question of turning and running, not with the mass of snarling, howling, sword-wielding warriors in front of them. The best they could do was to move back, fighting as they went, toward Duinifaire and the gate. Finally, they were on the edge of the gate, panting with the exertion they had already been through, as well as the press of the present battle.

Whether or not the Warriors saw the gate and hoped to kill them before they escaped, they did not know. They knew, however, that they were still fighting, striking, warding off blows as they backed through the gate.

The ground here was half a handbreadth higher than within the gate, and both of them stumbled. Fatha skipped to regain his balance, but Jochon's wounded leg gave out and he fell. One of the Wolf-warriors, coming through before the gate could be shut, stumbled himself, then began a downward killing blow at the fallen man.

Fatha was lunging forward, knowing already that he would be too late, when something whirred past him. The Warrior was half-turned by the impact, and slumped to the ground, his blow uncompleted. As the gate faded, Duinifaire walked over to retrieve his axe.

The little man, with help from Narolen, dealt with their wounds. While Grannon, who was still well wrapped up, lay quietly on the ground, watching with wide baby eyes what was going on around him.

When Duinifaire had finished dealing with Jochon's leg, Fatha spoke to him. "Duinifaire, can you explain all this to us?"

The little man shook his head. "It is not that I cannot. It is that there is one who will soon be coming to do the explaining, if I am not mistaken. Rather than have things told twice, best wait until she comes."

And indeed, as Narolen was putting the final touches to a bandage around Duinifaire's chest, there was a shimmer in the air beside them, and Nik-Malo walked through onto the hillside.

She bowed to them, and Duinifaire bowed low in return, wincing as the wound caught him.

“I have come to thank you, and to explain. If you will come sit by me, I will tell you the tale.”

They seated themselves, and she spoke. “Most of my folk, nixies and the like, concern themselves with studying what is and what might be. Occasionally, one studies simply what is, and occasionally such a one goes on then to decide what should be. The one with whom we were dealing was one of these.

“Having once decided what should be, and having sufficient power to make, or at least attempt to make things become as he had declared they should be, he then began to press the rest of us to fall in with his scheme.

“It was difficult to convince others of my kind to stand together to oppose him, for none of us like to be subservient to others, oftentimes extending that to the point of disliking advice which we know we should take. By the time there were several of us joined together against him, he had his defences arranged and secure, and need only wait with some patience for our alliance to begin to break.

“But I knew that he had as little patience as any other of our fellows, and if he saw a chance to put an end to things, he would do so. Thus I gave to you, Fatha, that jewel of mine, and managed to allow it to become known to him that I had secreted much of my power in a place where he could not find it.

“My hope was that he would begin to search for it, and that the search would force him to neglect his defences. Unfortunately for all of us, he was somewhat stronger even than I had guessed, and he was lucky in his search. He found it and he found you rapidly, and there was never a chance for us to break his defences.

"I sent Duinifaire to accompany you and to protect you, still hoping that as he was forced to try stronger and stronger measures to attack you, his defences must suffer."

She looked at Fatha. "I had no intent to use you as a mere tool; I hope you will believe that."

He looked back at her for a moment. "I believe it."

She nodded. "I chose to give my jewel to you, an outcast, because I had hoped to avoid just what happened in the end. An outcast, you see, ought to be someone for whom family and friendship mean little, and therefore, taking a hostage from that outcast in order to demand ransom would not seem worthwhile to our enemy.

"But you then demonstrated that an outcast might well love friends and family, and by the time we realized what his next move would surely be, it was too late.

"But when you came into his stronghold like that, bearing the jewel with you, then he was forced to take his mind away from his defences, allowing us to come in. So you served me better, in the end, than I had ever expected you to."

Fatha reached inside the breast of his armour coat to withdraw the jewel. "Since the need for it is gone, best you should have this back."

She accepted it. "As I said, you have served me better than I had ever expected you to. And because of that, the previous bargain, though it might stand, is unfair to you. I owe you a debt."

Fatha shook his head. "Nothing is owed to me, Lady. I did as I had promised."

She smiled. "And yet, let me do this much for you; let me send Duinifaire back with you, to be with your people so long as you live, to heal their hurts and diseases, to keep your animals well, inasmuch as it lies within his power. Will you take this from me?"

Fatha looked over at Duinifaire. "If he is willing to come, I am willing to have him."

"Oh yes, it is that I would be willing to come. It is that I have grown quite fond of you all."

Nik-Malo stood. "Good. It is agreed, then. And perhaps, from time to time, I shall visit you and your people, Fatha. Farewell, now." The air shimmered, and she was gone.

The others sat there for a while. Finally, Fatha stood and looked around.

"Well, if I am not mistaken, the city of Endolashan and the army of the Wanderpeople are in that direction, several hours' walk." He looked up at the sun. "We ought to be able to get there before dark, if we leave now."

Narolen picked up Grannon and stood up beside him. He put an arm around her shoulders and they set out.

* * *

Saskatoon, 31/10/88

Also by JP Wagner:

The Avantir Chronicles:

The Guardian of the Sword

The Crystal Crown

Talisman Series:

Stonecaller

Talisman of the Winds

Standalone:

The Search for the Unicorns

Railroad Rising: The Black Powder Rebellion

Maid of the Westermoor

Watch for more at J P Wagner's site.